SCAVENGERS IN SPACE

*by* ALAN E. NOURSE

# SCAVENGERS IN SPACE

DAVID McKAY COMPANY, Inc.     NEW YORK

Part of this book was published under
the title, "Gold in the Sky," in *Amazing
Science Fiction Stories*.

"Between Jupiter and Mars I will
put a planet...."

...Johannes Kepler (1571-1630)
(*Written before the discovery
of the Asteroid Belt*)

# CONTENTS

# SCAVENGERS IN SPACE

# PROLOGUE

---

ROGER HUNTER had completed his work long before the marauders appeared.

For two days now he had spent his waking hours down on the rock, prospecting it, taking samples of ore back to the little orbit ship for testing, doing the things that any miner in the Asteroid Belt would be expected to do. But he didn't really care what he found on the rock, because the important work was done. The incredible thing that he had found was hidden now, hidden and safe in a place that no one would think of searching, and that was all that mattered to Roger Hunter.

His treasure, he thought to himself as he worked. His big strike, safe now, until the time came to reveal it. He had not expected to find it when he had come out here the last time. He had never dreamed that such a thing was here, but when he found it he knew what he had to do.

It was on the second day that he saw the dark ship appear, moving in swiftly on contact course with his own ship. He

2

knew what it was the instant he saw it, long before the
golden triangle-and-J insignia became visible on its hull.

He dropped the samples he had been working with and
strapped himself quickly onto the scooter. He opened the
valve and saw the little asteroid drop away from him as he
moved swiftly up toward the loading lock of his ship. He
knew what his visitors wanted, he knew too well why they
were here.

Once in the control cabin he tore the roll of microfilm from
the camera he had been using and thrust it into the storage
bin. They would read it, of course, but it would have no
meaning to them. In the view screen he saw the dark ship
move closer, almost close enough for boarding.

Then he saw the leather gun case lying on the drafting
board, and his heart sank.

He picked it up, searching wildly for a place to hide it.
His eye stopped on his space pack lying on the floor, the
battered aluminum case he had used for so many years.
Quickly he threw open the lid, thrust the leather case under
the pile of clothing, and slammed the lid down again.

It was bad. If they searched it they might discover the
truth, but it was a risk he had to take.

For just a moment he thought of the boys and wondered if
he would ever see them again. Then he heard the lock crash
open somewhere below. Heavy boots pounded the corridor,
and three men walked into the control cabin.

Quietly, Roger Hunter turned to face them.

## Chapter One

### TROUBLE TIMES TWO

THE sun was glowing dull red as it slipped down behind the curving horizon of Mars, but Gregory Hunter was not able to see it.

There was no view screen in the ship's cabin; it was too tiny for that. Greg twisted around in the cockpit that had been built just big enough to hold him, and shifted his long legs against the brace-webbing, trying to get them comfortable. He took a deep breath and wrinkled his nose. Already the cabin was taking on the dank, musty smell of mechanically replaced air that made him think of the locker rooms and crowded gymnasiums of his school days. He shifted his legs again, fiddling with the straps across his chest to keep his hands from trembling.

His earphones crackled, and a familiar voice said, "Five minutes, Greg."

"Right." His own voice sounded harsh. He realized that he was frightened. Quickly he made the final check-through that he had rehearsed so many times in the past weeks. The straps

5

were all secure; he could reach the buttons on the control panel easily; and the handgrips felt right. He leaned back, forcing himself to relax, closing his eyes for a moment.

Here in the tiny experimental ship's cabin, he had no sense of time or motion, but he knew that the ship was clinging to its launching rack on the shell of the Star-Jump satellite station, spinning slowly in its twenty-four-hour orbit around Mars. Somewhere far below was the surface of the red planet itself, a huge dull-orange ball that filled the horizon from side to side.

Suddenly now, Greg wished he could see it for just a moment. Many times during his off-duty hours he had stood on the observation deck of the satellite station, watching the line of darkness crawl across Mars' surface. Sometimes, when the atmosphere was free of clouds, he could see the lights going on in Sun Lake City, Elysium, Poke's Hole, and a dozen other colony settlements dotting the equatorial surface of the planet. There were people down there . . . thousands of people . . . but here he was alone.

He knew he was afraid . . . but nobody else knew that, not even the captain waiting at the control board on the satellite, and in spite of the fear Greg Hunter would not have traded places at this moment with anyone else in the universe. He had worked too hard and waited too long for this moment.

He heard the count-down monitor clicking in his ears, and his hands clenched into fists. How far from Mars would he be ten minutes from now? He didn't know. Farther than any man had ever traveled before in the space of ten minutes, he knew, and faster. How far and how fast would depend on him alone. He gripped the handgrips, waiting.

"All set, Greg?" The captain's voice in the earphones cut into the silence.

"All set, Captain."

"You understand the program?"

Greg nodded. "Twenty-four hours out, twenty-four hours back, ninety degrees to the ecliptic, and all the acceleration I can stand both ways," he said slowly.

"That's right. But Greg—" the captain hesitated. "Don't overdo it. This is only a test run. We want you back in one piece."

Greg grinned to himself. He thought of the months of conditioning he had gone through to prepare for this run, the hours in the centrifuge to build up his tolerance to acceleration, the careful diet, the rigorous hours of physical conditioning. It was only one experiment, one tiny step in the work that could someday give men the stars, but to Gregory Hunter at this moment it was everything. "I'll be all right," he said.

"Good luck, then." The captain cut off, and the blast-off buzzer sounded.

Somewhere below, the ship's engines began to throb, a low steady vibration. The hum rose to a rumble, then to a roar. Like a giant hand pressing against his chest, the pressure began, growing heavier with every second. Greg's arms sagged against the straps; his legs felt like lead weights, and he could feel his lips pulling back as the acceleration increased. The scream of the engines grew higher as the weight bore down on him, pressing the air out of his lungs.

He was off. His heart hammered in his throat, and his eyes ached fiercely, but he paid no attention. His finger crept to the air-speed indicator, then to the cut-off switch. When the pressure became too great, when he began to black out, he would press it.

But not yet. Like a tiny metal dart, the ship was moving

away from the Star-Jump satellite, out into space, accelerating steadily. It was speed they wanted; they had to know how much acceleration a man could take for how long and still survive. It was up to him now to show them.

Fleetingly, he thought of Tom—poor old stick-in-the-mud Tom—working away in his grubby little Mars-bound laboratory, watching bacteria grow. Tom could never have qualified for a job like this. Tom couldn't even go into free-fall for ten minutes without getting sick all over the place. Greg felt a surge of pity for his brother, and then a twinge of malicious anticipation. Wait until Tom read the reports on *this* run! It was all right to spend your time poking around with bottles and test tubes if you couldn't do anything else, but it took something special to pilot an XP ship for Project Star-Jump. And after this run was over, even Tom would have to admit it.

There was a lurch, and quite suddenly the enormous pressure was gone. Greg took an unexpected gasp of air, felt his arms and legs rising up in reaction, out of control. He grabbed the shock bar, and stared down at the control panel.

Something was wrong. He hadn't pushed the cut-off button, yet the ship's engines were suddenly silent. He jabbed at the power switch. Nothing happened. Then the side jets spurted, and he was slammed sideways into the cot.

He snapped on the radio speaker. "Control ... can you read me? Something's gone wrong out here."

"Nothing's wrong," the captain's voice said in his earphones. "Just sit tight. I'm bringing you back in."

"Back!" Greg sat up against the webbing. "What do you mean?"

"Sorry, Greg. There's a call here from Sun Lake City. They

want you down there in a hurry. We'll have to scratch you
on this run."

"*Who* wants me down there?"

"The U.N. Council office. Signed by Major Briarton himself."

"But I *can't* go down to Mars now."

"Sorry. I can't argue with the major. We're bringing
you in."

Greg sank back, disappointment so thick he could taste
it in his mouth. Sun Lake City! That meant two days at
least, one down, one back, maybe more if connections
weren't right. It meant that the captain would send Morton
or one of the others out in his place. It meant. . . .

Suddenly he thought of what else it meant, and a chill
ran up his back. There was only one reason Major Briarton
would call him in like this. Something had happened to Dad.

Greg leaned back in the cot, suddenly tense. A thousand
frightful possibilities flooded his mind. It could only mean
that Dad was in some kind of trouble.

And if anything had happened to Dad. . . .

The sun was sinking rapidly toward the horizon when
the city finally came into sight in the distance, but try as he
would, Tom Hunter could not urge more than thirty-five
miles an hour from the huge lurching vehicle he was driving.

On an open paved highway the big pillow-wheeled
Sloppy Joe would do sixty in a breeze, but this desert route
was far from a paved road. Inside the pressurized passenger
cab, Tom gripped the shock bars with one arm and the other
leg, and jammed the accelerator to the floor. The engine
coughed, but thirty-five was all it would do.

Through the windshield Tom could see the endless rolling

dunes of the Martian desert stretching to the horizon on every side. They called Mars the red planet, but it was not red when you were close to it. There were multitudes of colors here—yellow, orange, brown, gray, occasional patches of gray-green—all shifting and changing in the fading sunlight. Off to the right were the worn-down peaks of the Mesabi II, one of the long, low mountain ranges of almost pure iron ore that helped give the planet its dull red appearance from outer space. And behind him, near the horizon, the tiny sun glowed orange out of a blue-black sky.

Tom fought the wheel as the Sloppy Joe jounced across a dry creek bed and swore softly to himself. Why hadn't he kept his head and waited for the mail ship that had been due at the lab to give him a lift back? He'd have been in Sun Lake City an hour ago. But the urgency of the message had driven caution from his mind. No information, no hint of what was wrong, just a single sentence telling him to come in to the city at once, by whatever means he had available.

Ten minutes later he had commandeered the Sloppy Joe and started out on the long cross-country run. A summons from the Mars Co-ordinator of the U.N. Interplanetary Council was the same as an order. But there was more to Tom's haste than that. There was only one reason that Major Briarton would be calling him in to Sun Lake City, and that reason meant trouble.

Something was wrong. Something had happened to Dad.

Now Tom peered up at the dark sky, squinting into the sun. Somewhere out there, between Mars and Jupiter, was a no man's land of danger, a great circling ring of space dirt and debris, the Asteroid Belt. And somewhere out there, Dad was working.

Tom thought for a moment of the pitiful little mining rig

that Dad had taken out to the belt; the tiny orbit ship to be used for headquarters and storage of the ore; the even tinier scout ship, Pete Racely's old *Scavenger* that he had sold to Roger Hunter for back taxes and repairs when he went broke in the belt looking for his big strike. It wasn't much of a mining rig for anybody to use, and the dangers of a small mining operation in the Asteroid Belt were frightening. It took skill to bring a little scout ship in for a landing on an asteroid rock hardly bigger than the ship itself; it took even more skill to rig the controlled Murexide charges to blast the rock into tiny fragments, and then run out the shiny magnetic net to catch the explosion debris and bring it in to the hold of the orbit ship.

Tom scowled, trying to shake off the feeling of uneasiness that was nibbling at his mind. Asteroid mining was dangerous, but Dad was no novice. Nobody on Mars knew how to handle a mining rig better than he did. He knew what he was doing out there, there was no real danger for him.

But what of the rumors that had found their way even to the obscurity of the outpost experimental lab where Tom was working?

Roger Hunter, a good man, a gentle and peaceful man, had finally seen all he could stomach of Jupiter Equilateral and its company mining policies six months before. He had told them so in plain, simple language when he turned in his resignation. They didn't try to stop him. A man was still free to quit a job on Mars if he wanted to, even a job with Jupiter Equilateral. But it was an open secret that the big mining outfit had not liked Hunter's way of resigning, taking half a dozen of their first-rate mining engineers with him. There had been veiled threats, rumors of attempts to close the markets to Hunter's ore, in open violation of U.N. Council policies on Mars.

Tom fought the wheel as the big tractor lumbered up another rise, and the huge plastic bubble of Sun Lake City came into view far down the valley below. Off to the right was the space port, with the tall spires of the shuttle ships rising up in sharp relief against the dark sky. One of the ships was landing now, settling down on a mushroom-shaped cloud of fire after its run out to the travel lanes where the huge interplanetary orbit ships made their endless circuits between Mars and Earth.

Tom clung to the shock bar and rode the tractor down the slope. Seeing the ships made him think of Greg. Had Greg been summoned too? He closed his lips tightly as a wave of anger passed through his mind. If anything had happened, no matter what, he thought, Greg would be there. Taking over and running things, as usual. He thought of the last time he had seen his brother, and then deliberately blocked out the engulfing bitterness. That had been more than a year ago. Maybe Greg had changed since then. But somehow, Tom didn't think so.

The Sloppy Joe was on the valley floor now, and ahead, the bubble covering the city was drawing closer. The sun was almost gone; lights were appearing inside the plastic shielding. Born and raised on Mars, Tom had seen the teeming cities of Earth only once in his life, but to him none of the splendors of the Earth cities could match the simple, quiet beauty of this Martian outpost settlement. There had been a time when people had said that Sun Lake City could never be built, that it could never survive if it were, but with each successive year it grew larger and stronger, the headquarters city for the planet that had become the new frontier of Earth.

The radiophone buzzed, and the airlock guard hailed him when he returned the signal. Tom gave his routine ID. He guided the tractor into the lock, waited until pressure and atmosphere rose to normal, and then leaped out of the cab.

Five minutes later he was walking across the lobby of the Interplanetary Council building, stepping into the down elevator. Three flights below, he stepped out into the office corridor of the U.N. Interplanetary Council on Mars.

If there was trouble, this was where he would find it.

He paused for a minute before the gray plastic door marked MAJOR FRANK BRIARTON in raised stainless steel letters. Then he pushed open the door and walked into the anteroom.

It was empty. At a desk in the corner an automatic typer was clicking busily, and green lights blinked on the secretary robot. "Yes, please? May I help you?" the metallic voice asked.

Tom picked up the speaker to answer and felt a touch on his shoulder. Behind him, a familiar voice said, "Hello, Twin."

At first glance they looked like carbon copies of each other, although they were no more identical than identical twins ever are. Greg stood a good two inches taller than Tom. His shoulders were broad, and there was a small gray scar over one eye that stood out in contrast to the healthy tanned color of his face. Tom was of slighter build, and wirier, his skin much more pale.

But they had the same dark hair, the same gray eyes, the same square, stubborn line to the jaw. They looked at each other for a moment without speaking. Then Greg grinned and clapped his brother on the shoulder.

"So you got here, finally," he said. "I was beginning to think I'd have to go out on the desert and find you."

"Oh, I got here, all right," Tom said. "I see you did too."

"Yes," Greg said heavily. "Can't argue with the major, you know."

"What does he want?"

"How should I know? All he said was to get down here fast. And now he isn't even here himself, and his squawk box here isn't any help."

The secretary robot was repeating its mechanical question for the fourth time. Greg kicked at the foot pedal, cutting it off in mid-sentence. "Whatever he wants, it had better be good. Of all the times to drag me down here."

"Well, *something's* happened, that's sure.'

"Like what?" Greg snapped. "For three months I've been working to take that ship out, and now they've sent Morton out in my place. Well, now I'm here. There had just better be a good reason."

"Is Dad on Mars?' Tom asked.

Greg looked at him. "I don't know."

"We could check the register."

"I've already checked it. He hasn't logged in, but that doesn't mean anything."

"I suppose not," Tom said glumly.

They were silent for a moment. Then, "Look, what are you worried about?" Greg asked. "Nothing could have happened to Dad. He's been mining the belt for years."

"I know. I just wish he were here, that's all. If he's in some kind of trouble . . . ."

"What kind of trouble? You're looking for spooks."

"Spooks like Jupiter Equilateral, maybe," Tom said. "They could make plenty of trouble for Dad."

"With the U.N. in the driver's seat here? They wouldn't dare. Why do you think the major rides them so hard with all the claim-filing regulations? He'd give his right arm for a chance to break that outfit into pieces."

"I still wish somebody had gone out to the belt with Dad," Tom said.

"You mean somebody like me?"

"I didn't say that."

"Well, why me?" Greg said angrily. "You think just because you always need somebody to look after you that everybody else does, too. Dad doesn't need a baby sitter." He broke off and jammed his hands in his pockets. "All right, maybe one of us should have gone with him, I don't know. But if he's gotten into trouble, having one of us around wouldn't have made any difference anyway. You know Dad as well as I do—"

He broke off as the door opened. The newcomer was a tall, gray-haired man with U.N. Council stripes on his lapel, and major's rockets on his shoulders. "Sorry I'm late, boys," Major Briarton said. "I'd hoped to be here when you arrived." He pulled off his cap and gloves and looked up at the twins. "Now, then, what were we shouting at each other about?"

"Nothing," Greg said, flushing.

"Well, come on in and sit down." The major led them into the inner office and sank down behind his desk. He seemed thinner now than when Tom had seen him last; his eyes looked tired, and his face was heavily lined. "I'm sorry to have to pull you in here like this, but I'm afraid I had no choice. When did you boys hear from your father last?"

They looked at each other. "I saw him six weeks ago," Tom said. "Just before he left to go out to the belt again."

"Nothing since then?"

"Not a word."

The major chewed his lip. "Greg?"

"I had a note at Christmas, I think. But what—"

"What did he say in the note?"

"He said Merry Christmas and Happy New Year. Dad isn't much of a letter writer."

"Nothing at all about what he was doing?"

Greg shook his head. "Look, Major, if there's some sort of trouble—"

"Yes, I'm afraid there's trouble," the major said. He looked at them and spread his hands helplessly. "There isn't any easy way to tell you, but you've got to know. There's been an accident, out in the belt."

"Accident?" Greg said.

"A very serious accident. A fuel tank exploded in the scooter your father was riding back to the *Scavenger*. It must have been very sudden, and by the time help arrived—" the major broke off, unable to find words.

For a long moment there was utter silence in the room. Outside, an elevator was buzzing, and a typewriter clicked monotonously somewhere in the building.

Then Tom Hunter broke the silence. "Who was it, Major?" he asked. "Who was it that killed our father?"

## Chapter Two

## JUPITER EQUILATERAL

FOR a moment, Major Briarton just stared at him. Then he was on his feet, shaking his head as he came around the desk. "Tom, use your head," he said. "It's as much of a shock to me as it is to you, but you can't afford to jump to false conclusions."

Tom looked up bitterly. "He's dead, isn't he?"

"Yes, he's dead. He must have died the instant of the explosion."

"You mean you don't know?"

"I wasn't there at the time it happened; no."

"Then who was?"

Major Briarton again spread his hands helplessly. "Nobody was. Your father was alone. From what we could tell later, he'd left the *Scavenger* to land on one of his claims, using the ship's scooter for the landing. He was on the way back to the *Scavenger* when the rear tank exploded. There wasn't enough left of it to tell what went wrong, but it was an accident; there was no evidence to suggest anything else."

17

Tom looked at him. "You really believe that?"

"I can only tell you what we found."

"Well, I don't believe it for a minute," Tom said angrily. "How long have you and Dad been friends? Twenty years? Twenty-five? Longer than we've been alive, that's sure. Do you really think Dad could have an accident with a mining rig?"

"I know he was an expert engineer," the major said. "But things can happen that even an expert can't foresee, mining in the belt."

"Things like a fuel tank exploding? Not to Dad, they wouldn't happen. I don't care what anybody says."

"Easy, Tom," Greg said.

"Well, I won't take it easy! Dad was too careful for something like that to happen. If he had an accident, somebody *made* it happen."

Greg turned to the major. "What was Dad doing out there?"

"Mining."

"By himself? No crew at all?"

"No, he was alone."

"I thought the regulations said there always had to be at least two men working an asteroid claim."

"That's right. Your father had Johnny Coombs with him when he left Sun Lake City. They signed out as a team, and then Johnny came back to Mars on the first shuttle ship."

"How come?"

"Not even Johnny knows. Your father just sent him back, and there was nothing we could do about it then. The U.N. has no jurisdiction in the belt, unless a major crime has been committed." Major Briarton shook his head. "If a man is determined to mine a claim all by himself out there, he can find a dozen different ways to wiggle out of the regulations."

"But Dad would never be that stupid," Greg said. "If he was alone when it happened, who found him?"

"A routine U.N. patrol ship. When your father failed to check in at the regular eight-hour signal, they went out to see what was wrong. But by the time they reached him, it was too late to help."

"I just don't get it," Greg said. "Dad had more sense than to try to mine out there all by himself."

"I know," the major said. "But I don't know the answer. I had the patrol ship go over the scene of the accident with a fine tooth comb after they reported what had happened, but there was nothing there to find. It was an accident, and that's that."

"What about Jupiter Equilateral?" Tom said hotly. "Everybody knows they were out to get Dad. Why don't you find out what *they* were doing when it happened, bring *them* in for questioning?"

"I can't do that," the major said wearily.

"Why can't you?"

"I haven't a scrap of evidence."

"But you're the Mars Co-ordinator, aren't you?" Tom persisted. "You act like you're scared of them."

Major Briarton's lips tightened angrily. "All right, since you put it that way. I *am* scared of them. They're big, and they're powerful. If they had their way, there wouldn't be any United Nations control on Mars, there wouldn't be *anybody* to fight them and keep them in check. There wouldn't be any independent miners out in the belt, either, because they'd all be bought out or dead, and Earth would pay through the nose for every ounce of metal that she got from the Asteroid Belt. That company has been trying to drive the U.N. off Mars for thirty years, and they've come so close to it that it scares me plenty." He paused, then went on. "And that is exactly why I refuse to stir up a mess over this thing, unhappy as it is, without something more than suspicions and rumors to back me up, because all Jupiter Equilateral needs is one big issue to make us look like fools out here, and we're through."

He crossed the room to a wall cabinet, opened it, and pulled out a scarred aluminum box. "We found this in the cabin of the *Scavenger*. I thought you boys might want it."

They both recognized it instantly. It was the battered old spacer's pack that Roger Hunter had used for as long as they could remember. It seemed to them, suddenly, as if a part of him had appeared here in the room with them. Greg looked at the box and turned away. "You open it," he said to Tom in a sick voice.

There was nothing much inside—some clothing, a pipe and tobacco pouch, a jackknife, half a dozen other items so familiar that Tom could hardly bear to touch them. At the bottom of the pack was the heavy leather gun case which had always held Roger Hunter's ancient .44 revolver. Tom dropped it back without even opening the flap. He closed the box and took a deep breath. "Then you really believe that it was an accident and nothing more?" he said to the major.

"All the evidence points to it. There was nothing to indicate anything else."

"I'm not talking about evidence, now. I'm talking about what you think."

Major Briarton shook his head. "What I think or don't think doesn't make any difference. It just doesn't matter. In order to do anything, I've got to have evidence, and there just isn't any evidence. I can't even take a ship out there for a second look, with the evidence I have, and that's all there is to it."

"But you think that maybe it wasn't an accident, just the same," Tom pursued.

The major hesitated. Then he shook his head again. "I'm sorry, but I've got to stand on what I've said. And I think you'd better stand on it, too."

It should have been enough, but it wasn't. As Tom Hunter walked with his brother down the broad upper ramp to the business section of Sun Lake City, he could not shake off the feeling of helpless anger, the growing conviction that Dad's death involved something more than the tragic accident in space that Major Briarton had insisted it was.

"He didn't tell us everything he knew," Tom said fiercely. "He didn't say everything he wanted to say, either. He doesn't think it was an accident any more than I do."

"We can't put words in his mouth," Greg said. "And anyway, you shouldn't have badgered him like that. He was only doing what he had to do, and you didn't help him out any."

"He didn't believe a word he was saying," Tom said.

"How do you know? Are you a mind reader?"

"No."

"Well, Dad wasn't a superman, either. He was taking an awful risk, trying to work a mining rig by himself, and he had a bad break. Why do you have to have somebody to blame for it?"

"Keep talking," Tom said. "You'll convince yourself yet."

Greg just jammed his hands in his pockets, and they

walked on in silence. On the second level of the Martian underground city, stores and supply depots had crowded out the living quarters, and the corridors were busy with people. The low oxygen concentration and the low pressure of Mars' atmosphere had proven unsuitable for human life except for very brief periods of exposure; every human habitation on Mars depended on the protective plastic bubble outside to keep in the artificially maintained atmosphere. As a consequence, the cities on Mars had never spread out on the surface like Earth cities, but were excavated into the ground, and resembled huge multi-unit apartment buildings, with ramps and concourses connecting the various levels and segments of the city.

Of all the Martian cities, Sun Lake City was the biggest, the busiest, the noisiest. Already it was crowded with miners and their families, prospectors, rocket men, research men and builders, and for the third time in a decade the power machinery was at work excavating for another level of the city to make room for more.

For Tom and Greg Hunter, Sun Lake City had always been home. Now they walked along the main concourse, Tom with the aluminum box under his arm, Greg with his own spacer's pack thrown over his shoulder. They didn't talk; rather than being drawn closer by the news of the tragedy, it seemed that they had drawn farther apart, as though the one common link that had held them together had suddenly been broken.

They turned into the dining commissary, mingling with the crowd as people poured up from the living quarters and offices on the lower levels. They stood across from each other at the table, picking at their food and saying nothing. Finally

Tom tossed down his fork. "At least there's one thing we can do," he said. "I'm going to call Johnny Coombs."

He weaved through the crowd of diners to the phone booths in the rear and dialed a number. Johnny had been a friend of the family for years; he and Roger Hunter had been partners in many mining ventures in the Asteroid Belt before Hunter had taken his position with Jupiter Equilateral. If Johnny had any suspicions that Roger Hunter's accident had been more than an accident, he certainly would not hesitate to voice them.

After a dozen rings, Tom hung up, tried another number. There was no answer there, either. Frowning, Tom rang the city's central paging system. "Put in a personal call for Johnny Coombs," he said when the "record" signal flashed on. "Tell him to contact the Hunters when he comes in. We'll be at home."

Back at the table, he finished his dinner without tasting it. Greg checked his watch, and together they started for the down ramp that lead to the living quarters of the city. A jitney passed them, loaded with people bound for quarters, but neither of them made a move to hop on. When they reached H wing on the fourth level, they turned right down an apartment corridor, and stopped in front of a familiar doorway. Tom pressed his palm against the lock plate, and the door swung open.

It was home to them, the only home they had ever known. Soft lights sprang up on the walls of the apartment as the door opened. Tom saw the old bookcases lining the walls, the drafting board and light at the far end of the room, the simple chairs and dining table, the door which led into the bedroom and kitchen beyond. The room still had the slightly disheveled look it had had ever since Mom died—a slipper on the floor here, a book face down on the couch there. It looked as though Dad had just stepped out for an hour or so. . . .

Tom was three steps into the room before he saw the visitor. The man was sitting comfortably in Roger Hunter's easy chair, a short, fat man with round pink cheeks that sagged a little and a double chin that rested on his neck scarf. There were two other men in the room, both large and broad-shouldered; one of them nodded to the fat man, and moved to stand between the twins and the door.

The fat man was out of his seat before the boys could speak, smiling at them and holding out his hand. "I wanted to be sure to see you before you left the city," he was saying, "so we just came on in to wait. I hope you don't mind our butting in, so to speak." He chuckled, looking from one twin to the other. "You don't know me, I suppose. I'm Merrill Tawney. Representing Jupiter Equilateral, you know."

Tom took the card he was holding out, looked at the name and the tiny gold symbol in the corner, a J in the center of a triangle. He handed the card to Greg. "I've seen you before," he told the fat man. "What do you want with us?"

Tawney smiled again, spreading his hands. "We've heard about the tragedy, of course. Shocking. . . . Roger was one of our group so recently. We wanted you to know that if there is anything at all we can do to help, we'd be only too glad."

"Thanks," Greg said. "But we're doing just fine."

Tawney's smile tightened a little, but he hung on to it. "I always felt close to your father," he said. "All of us at Jupiter Equilateral did. We were all sorry to see him leave."

"I bet you were," Greg said, "he was the best mining

engineer you ever had. But Dad could never stand liars, or crooked ways of doing business."

One of the men started for Greg, but the fat man stopped him with a wave of his hand. "We had our differences of opinion," he said. "We saw things one way, your father saw them another way. But he was a fine man, one of the finest."

"Look, Mr. Tawney, you'd better say what you came to say and get out of here," Greg said angrily, "before we give your friends here something to do."

"I merely came to offer you some help," Tawney said. He was no longer smiling. "Since your father's death, you two have acquired certain responsibilities. I thought we might relieve you of some of them."

"What sort of responsibilities?"

"You have an unmanned orbit ship which is now a derelict in the Asteroid Belt. You have a scout ship out there also. You can't just leave them there as a navigation hazard to every ship traveling in the sector. There are also a few mining claims which aren't going to be of much value to you now."

"I see," Greg said. "Are you offering to buy Dad's mining rig?"

"Well, I doubt very much that we'd have any use for it, as such. But we could save you the trouble of going out there to haul it in."

"That's very thoughtful," Greg said. "How much are you offering?"

Tom looked up in alarm. "Wait a minute," he said. "That rig's not for sale."

"How much?" Greg repeated.

"Forty thousand dollars," Merrill Tawney said. "Ship, rig and claims. We'll even pay the transfer tax."

Tom stared at the man, wondering if he had heard right. He knew what Dad had paid for the rig; he had been with him when the papers were signed. Tawney's offer was three times as much as the rig was worth.

But Greg was shaking his head. "I don't think we could sell at that price."

The fat man's hands fluttered. "You understand that those ships are hardly suited to a major mining operation like ours," he said, "and the claims. . . ." He dismissed them with a wave of his hand. "Still, we'd want you to be happy with the price. Say, forty-five thousand?"

Greg hesitated, shook his head again. "I guess we'd better think it over, Mr. Tawney."

"Fifty thousand is absolutely the top," Tawney said sharply. "I have the papers right here, drawn up for your signatures, but I'm afraid we can't hold the offer open."

"I don't know, we might want to do some mining ourselves," Greg said. "For all we know, Dad might have struck some rich ore on one of those claims."

Tawney laughed. "I hardly think so. Those claims were all Jupiter Equilateral rejects. Our own engineers found nothing but low-grade ore on any of them."

"Still, it might be fun to look."

"It could be very expensive fun. Asteroid mining is a dangerous business, even for experts. For amateurs—" Tawney spread his hands—"accidents occur."

"Yes, we've heard about those accidents," Greg said coldly. "I don't think we're quite ready to sell, Mr. Tawney. We may never be ready to sell to you, so don't stop breathing until we call you. Now if there's nothing more, why don't you take your friends and go somewhere else?"

The fat man scowled; he started to say something, then saw the look on Greg's face, and shrugged. "I'd advise you to give my offer some careful thought," he said as he started for the door. "It might be very foolish for you to try to use that rig."

Smiling, Greg closed the door in his face. Then he turned and winked at Tom. "Great fellow, Mr. Tawney. He almost had me sold."

"So I noticed," Tom said. "For a while I thought you were serious."

"Well, we found out how high they'd go. That's a very generous outfit Mr. Tawney works for."

"Or else a very crooked one," Tom said. "Are you wondering the same thing I'm wondering?"

"Yes," Greg said slowly. "I think I am."

"Then that makes three of us," a heavy voice rumbled from the bedroom door.

Johnny Coombs was a tall man, so thin he was almost gangling, with a long nose, and shaggy eyebrows jutting out over his eyes. With his rudely cropped hair and his huge hands, he looked like a caricature of a frontier Mars farmer, but the blue eyes under the eyebrows were not dull.

He grinned at the boys' surprise, and walked into the room. "You don't mind if I have a seat, I hope," he said in his deep bass voice. "I been standin' there inside that door for almost an hour, and I'm tired of standin'."

"Johnny!" Tom cried. "We were trying to find you."

"I know," Johnny said. "So were a lot of other people, includin' your friends there."

"Well, did you hear what Tawney wanted?"

"I'm not so quick on my feet any more," Johnny Coombs said, "but I got nothin' wrong with my ears." He scratched his jaw and looked up sharply at Greg. "Not many people nowadays get a chance to bargain with Merrill Tawney."

Greg shrugged. "He named a price and I didn't like it."

"Three times what the rig is worth," Coombs said.

"That's what I didn't like," Greg said. "That outfit wouldn't give us a break like that just for old times' sake. Do you think they would?"

"Well, I don't know," Johnny said slowly. "Back before they built the city here, they used to have rats getting into the grub. Came right down off the ships. Got rid of most of them, finally, but it seems to me we've still got some around, even if they've got different shapes now." He jerked his thumb toward the bedroom door. "In case you're wondering, that's why I was standin' back there all this time, just to make sure you didn't sell out to Tawney no matter what price he offered."

Tom jumped up excitedly. "Then you know something about Dad's accident!"

"No, I can't say I do. I wasn't there."

"Do you really think it was an accident?"

"Can't prove it wasn't."

"But at least you've got some ideas," Tom said.

Johnny Coombs stood up and started the coffee-mix heating on the stove. "Takes more than ideas to make a case," he said at length. "But there's one thing I do know. I've got no proof, not a shred of it, but I'm sure of one thing just as sure as I'm on Mars." He looked at the twins thoughtfully. "Your dad wasn't just prospecting, out in the belt. He'd run onto something out there, something big."

The twins stared at him. "Run unto something?" Greg said. "You mean. . . ."

"I mean I think your dad hit a big strike out there, rich metal, a real bonanza lode, maybe the biggest strike that's ever been made," the miner said slowly. "And then somebody got to him before he could bring it in."

*Chapter Three*

---

## TOO MANY WARNINGS

FOR a moment, neither of the boys could say anything at all. From the time they had learned to talk, they had heard stories and tales that the miners and prospectors told about the big strike, the pot of gold at the end of the rainbow, the wonderful, elusive goal of every man who had ever taken a ship out into the Asteroid Belt.

For almost a hundred and fifty years—since the earliest days of space exploration—there had been miners prospecting in the asteroids. Out there, beyond the orbit of Mars and inside the orbit of Jupiter, were a hundred thousand—maybe a hundred million, for all anybody knew—chunks of rock, metal and debris, spinning in silent orbit around the sun. Some few of the asteroids were big enough to be called planets—Ceres, five hundred miles in diameter; Juno, Vesta, Pallas, half a dozen more. A few thousand others, ranging in size from ten to a hundred miles in diameter, had been charted and followed in their orbits by the observatories, first from Earth's airless Moon, then from Mars. There were tens of thousands more that had never been charted. Together they made up the Asteroid Belt, spread out in space like a broad road around the sun, echoing the age-old call of the bonanza.

For there was wealth in the asteroids, wealth beyond a man's wildest dreams, if only he could find it.

Earth, with its depleted iron ranges, its exhausted tin and copper mines, and its burgeoning population, was hungry for metal. Earth needed steel, tin, nickel, and zinc; more than anything, Earth needed ruthenium, the rare earth catalyst that made the huge solar energy converters possible.

Mars was rich in the ores of these metals, but the ores were buried deep in the ground. The cost of mining them, and of lifting the heavy ore from Mars' gravitational field and carrying it to Earth was prohibitive. Only the finest carbon steel, and the radioactive metals, smelted and purified on Mars and transported to Earth, could be made profitable.

But from the Asteroid Belt, it was a different story. There was no gravity to fight on the tiny asteroids. On these chunks of debris, the metals lay close to the surface, easy to mine. Ships orbiting in the belt could fill their holds with their precious metal cargoes and transfer them in space to the interplanetary orbit ships spinning back toward Earth. It was hard work, and dangerous. Most of the ore was low-grade, and brought little return. But always there was the lure of the big strike, the lode of almost pure metal that could bring a fortune to the man who found it.

A few such strikes had been made. Forty years before, a single claim had brought its owner seventeen million dollars in two years. A dozen other men had stumbled onto fortunes in the belt, but such metal-rich fragments were grains of sand in a mighty river. For every man who found one, a thousand others spent years looking and then perished in the fruitless search.

And now Johnny Coombs was telling them that their father had been one of that incredible few.

They stared at the tall, lanky miner while he poured himself a cup of coffee. Then Greg laughed. "Johnny, you're crazy," he said. "You were telling us tales about the big strikes when we were five years old. I didn't believe you then, and I don't believe you now."

Johnny Coombs looked at him soberly. "Stories for the kiddies are one thing. This is something else. I'm speakin' the truth, boy."

"You think Dad hit a bonanza lode out there?"

"That's what I said."

"Did you see it with your own eyes?"

"No."

"You weren't even out there with him!"

"No."

"Then why are you so sure he found something?"

"Because he told me so," Johnny Coombs said quietly.

The boys looked at each other. "He actually *said* he'd found a rich lode?" Tom asked eagerly.

"Not exactly," Johnny said. "Matter of fact, he never actually told me *what* he'd found. He needed somebody to sign aboard the *Scavenger* with him in order to get a clearance to blast off, but he never did plan to take me out there with him. 'I can't take you now, Johnny,' he told me. 'I've found something out there, but I've got to work it alone for a while.' I asked him what he'd found, and he just gave me that funny little grin of his and said, 'Never mind what it is, it's big enough for both of us. You just keep your mouth shut, and you'll find out soon enough.' And then he wouldn't say another word until we were homin' in on the shuttle ship to drop me off."

Johnny finished his coffee and pushed the cup aside. "I knew he wasn't jokin'. He was excited, and I think he was scared, too. Just before I left him, he said, 'There's one other thing, Johnny. Things might not work out quite the way I figure them, and if they don't, make sure the twins know what I've told you.' I told him I would, and headed back. That was the last I heard from him until the patrol ship found him floating in space with a torn-open suit and a ruined scooter floating a few miles away."

They sat in silence for a while. Then Tom said, "Do you think that Jupiter Equilateral knew Dad had found something?"

"Who knows? I'm sure that *he* never told them, but it's awful hard to keep a secret like that, and they sound mighty eager to buy that rig," Johnny Coombs said.

"Yes, and it doesn't make sense. I mean, if they were responsible for Dad's accident, why didn't they just check in for him on schedule and then quietly bring in their rig to jump the claim?"

"Maybe they couldn't find it," Johnny said. "If they'd killed your dad, they wouldn't have dared hang around very long right then. Even if they'd kept the signal going, a patrol ship might have come into the region any time. And if a U.N. patrol ship ever caught them working a dead man's claim without reporting the dead man, the suit would really start to leak." Johnny shook his head. "Remember, your dad had a dozen claims out there. They might have had to scout the whole works to find the right one. Much easier to do it out in the open, with your signatures on a claim transfer. But one thing is sure—if they *knew* what Roger found out there, and where it was, Tawney would never be offerin' you triple price for the rig."

"Then whatever Dad found is still out there," Tom said.

"I'd bet my last dime on it."

"There might even be something to show that the accident wasn't an accident," Tom went on. "Something even the major would have to admit was evidence."

Johnny Coombs pursed his lips. "Might be," he conceded.

"Well, what are we waiting for? We turned Tawney's offer down; he might be sending a crew out to jump the claim right now."

"If he hasn't already," Johnny said.

"Then we've got to get out there."

"With what?" Greg broke in. "I think we ought to get out there, too, but let's face facts. It costs plenty to outfit a trip into the belt, and I don't have that kind of money."

"Neither do I," Johnny Coombs admitted. "Still, we might not need too much. There are a lot of miners on Mars who thought Roger Hunter was a pretty fine guy. They might just kick in to outfit us."

"But even so, what could we do?" Greg said. "I don't know anything about asteroid mining."

"I do. You could pilot us out and handle the navigation, and as for Tom—"

"As for Tom, he could get sick all over the place and keep us busy just taking care of him," Greg said sourly. "You and me, yes. Not Tom. You don't know that boy in a space ship."

Tom started to his feet, glaring at his brother. "That's got nothing to do with it."

"It's true, isn't it? You'd be a big help out there."

Johnny looked at Tom. "You always get sick in free-fall?" Tom nodded miserably.

"Even with dramamine?"

"I always have. But I can control it if I try."

"Look, let's be reasonable," Greg said. "You'd just be in the way. There are plenty of things you could do right here, and Johnny and I could handle the rig alone."

Tom faced his brother angrily. "If you think I'm going to stay here and keep myself company, you're crazy," he said. "This is one show you're not going to run, so just quit trying. If you go out there, I go."

Greg shrugged. "Okay, Twin. It's your stomach, not mine."

"Then let me worry about it."

"I hope," Johnny said, "that that's the worst we have to worry about. Maybe it is—but I doubt it. Merrill Tawney is fat, but he's no fool. If we try a trip out there, he may go quite a way to stop us. And if he does, we're goin' to have plenty of fightin' to do without fightin' each other." He looked from one to the other. "Okay?"

"Okay," Greg said, after a moment. Tom nodded.

"Then let's get started plannin'."

Time was the factor uppermost in their minds. They knew that even under the best of conditions, it could take weeks to outfit and prepare for a run out to the belt. A ship had to be leased and fueled; there were supplies to lay in. There was the problem of clearance to take care of, claims to be verified and spotted, orbit co-ordinates to be computed and checked

—a thousand details to be dealt with, any one of which might delay embarkation from an hour to a day or more.

It was not surprising that Tom and Greg were dubious when Johnny told them they could be ready to clear ground in less than twenty-four hours. Even knowing that Merrill Tawney might already have a mining crew at work on Roger Hunter's claims, they could not believe that the red tape of preparation and clearance could be cut away so swiftly.

They underestimated Johnny Coombs.

Six hours after he left them, he was back with a signed lease giving them the use of a scout ship and fuel to take them out to the belt and back again; the ship was in the Sun Lake City racks waiting for them whenever they were ready.

"What kind of a ship?" Greg wanted to know.

"A Class III Flying Dutchman with overhauled atomics and hydrazine side jets," Johnny said, waving the transfer order. "Think you can fly it?"

Greg whistled. "Can I! I trained in a Dutchman; just about the fastest scouter there is. What condition?"

"Lousy. But it's fueled, with six weeks' supplies in the hold, and it doesn't cost us a cent. Courtesy of a friend. It'll do, but you'll have to check it over."

They inspected the ship, a weather-beaten scouter that looked like a relic of the nineties. Inside there were signs of many refittings and overhauls, but the atomics were well shielded, and it carried a surprisingly large chemical fuel auxiliary for the size of the cabin. Greg disappeared into the engine room, and Tom and Johnny left him testing valves and circuits while they headed down to the U.N. registry office in the control tower.

On the way Johnny outlined the remaining outfitting steps.

Tom would be responsible for getting the clearance permit through registry; Johnny would check out all supplies, and then contact the observatory for the orbit co-ordinates of Roger Hunter's claims.

"I thought the orbits were mapped on the claim papers," Tom said. "I mean, every time an asteroid is claimed, the orbit has to be charted."

"That's right, but the orbit goes all the way around the sun. We know where the *Scavenger* was when the patrol ship found her, but she's been traveling in orbit ever since. The observatory computer will pinpoint her for us and chart a collision course so we can cut out and meet her instead of trailin' her for a week. Do you have the crew papers Greg and I signed?"

"Right here."

They were stepping off the ramp below the ship when a man loomed up out of the shadows. He was a miner Tom had never seen before. Johnny nodded as he approached. "Any news, Jack?"

"Quiet as a church," said the man.

"We'll be held up another eight hours at least," Johnny said. "Don't go to sleep on us, Jack."

"Don't worry about us sleepin'," the man said grimly. "There's been nobody around but yourselves, so far, except the clearance inspector."

Johnny looked up sharply. "You check his papers?"

"*And* his prints. He was all right."

Johnny took Tom's arm, and they headed through the gate toward the control tower. "I guess I'm just naturally suspicious," he grinned, "but I'd sure hate to have a broken cut-off switch, or a fuel valve go out of whack at just the wrong moment."

"You think Tawney would dare to try something here?" Tom asked.

"Never hurts to check. We'll have our hands full for a few hours getting set, so I just asked my friends to keep an eye on things. Always did say that a man who's goin' to gamble is smart to cover his bets."

At the control tower they parted, and Tom walked in to the clearance office. Johnny's watchman had startled him; for the first time he felt a chill of apprehension. If they were right—if this trip to the belt were not a wild goose chase from the very start—then Roger Hunter's accident had been no accident at all.

Quite suddenly, Tom felt very thankful that Johnny Coombs had friends.

"I don't like it," the major said, facing Tom and Greg across the desk in the U.N. registry office below the control tower. "You've gotten an idea in your heads, and you just won't listen to reason."

Somewhere above them, Tom could hear the low-pitched rumble of a scout ship blasting from its launching rack. "All we want to do is go out and work Dad's claim," he said for the second time.

"I know perfectly well what you want to do. That's why I told the people here to alert me if you tried to clear a ship. You don't know what you're doing, and I'm not going to sign those clearance papers."

"Why not?" Greg asked.

"Because you're going out there asking for trouble, that's why not."

"But you told us before that there wasn't any trouble. Dad

had an accident, that was all. So how could we get in trouble?"

"I won't even discuss it with you," the major snapped. "I'm simply refusing you clearance."

Greg shook his head. "I don't think you can do that, Major. We're both past eighteen, birthday was last March. We're of legal age, so you can't object to that. We're not prospecting, we're heading out for claimed rocks. Those were Dad's claims, and they were free and clear. We have a spaceworthy craft to take us out there, and a qualified rig waiting for us when we get there. We have more than a minimum crew signed. Maybe I sound like a space lawyer, but I'd like to know what regulation you're going to use to stop us."

The major's face was an angry red. He started to say something, then stopped, and scowled at them instead. They met his stare. Finally he threw up his hands. "All right, so legally I can't stop you," he said. "But at least I can beg you to use your heads. You're wasting time and money on a foolish idea. You're walking into dangers and risks that you can't handle, and I hate to see it happen."

"What kind of dangers?" Greg said.

"Mining in the belt is a job for experienced men, not rank novices."

"Johnny Coombs is no novice."

"No, but he's lost his wits, taking you two out there."

"Well, are there any other dangers you have in mind?"

Once more the major searched for words, and failed to find them. "No," he sighed, "and you wouldn't listen if I did."

"It seems everybody is warning us about how dangerous this trip is likely to be," Greg said quietly. "Last night it was Merrill Tawney. He offered to buy us out; he was so eager for a deal that he offered us a fantastic price. Then Johnny tells us that Dad hit some rich ore when he was out there on his last trip, but never got a chance to bring it in because of his ... accident. Up until now I haven't been so sure Dad *didn't* just have an accident, but now I'm beginning to wonder. Too many people have been warning us."

"You're determined to go out there, then?"

"That's about right."

The major picked up the clearance papers, glanced at them quickly, and signed them. "All right, you're cleared. I hate to do it, but I suppose I'd go with you if the law would let me. And I'll tell you one thing—if you can find a single particle of evidence that will link Jupiter Equilateral or anybody else to your father's death, I'll use all the power I have to break them across my knee." He handed the papers back to Tom. "But be careful, because if Jupiter Equilateral is involved in it, they're going to play dirty. If there's something they want badly enough, they won't waste much time with you. So watch out."

At the door he turned. "Good trip, and good luck."

Tom folded the papers and stuck them thoughtfully in his pocket.

The Hunters met Johnny Coombs in the registry offices upstairs; Tom patted his pocket happily. "We're cleared in forty-five minutes," he said.

Johnny grinned. "Then we're all set." They headed up the ramp, reached ground level, and started out toward the launching racks.

At the far end of the field a powerful Class I Ranger, one of the Jupiter Equilateral scout fleet, was settling down into its slot in a perfect landing maneuver. The triangle-and-J insignia gleamed brightly on her dark hull. She was a rich, luxurious-looking ship; in comparison, the Class III Dutchman looked small and shabby, its hull pitted and scarred by meteors and dust. The Ranger, with her dozens of sister ships, made a formidable fleet in the Asteroid Belt. With that fleet, Jupiter Equilateral had built its strength as a mining concern in the belt; the Ranger had power, and maneuverability, and a highly trained crew to handle her.

But with that power there was a touch of arrogance. Many miners on Mars could remember when Jupiter Equilateral had been nothing more than a tiny mining company working claims in the remote "equilateral" cluster of asteroids far out in Jupiter's orbit. Gradually the company had grown and flourished, accumulating wealth and power as it grew, leaving behind it a thousand half-confirmed stories of cheating, piracy, murder and theft. Other small mining outfits had fallen by the wayside until now over two-thirds of all asteroid mining claims were held by Jupiter Equilateral, and the small independent miners were forced more and more to take what was left, what Jupiter Equilateral didn't want.

They reached the gate to the Dutchman's launching slot, and the watchman hailed them. "Not a sign of anythin'" he said, with a touch of disappointment in his voice, "and me all set for a good brawl."

Johnny chewed his lip thoughtfully. "Well, thanks anyway. You took a weight off our minds."

The man watched them start up the ramp for the ship. "Johnny," he said suddenly, "if you need any more crew, just speak up." He jerked a thumb toward the Ranger that had just landed. "There's plenty of boys around here who'd like to tangle with that crew."

"Thanks, Jack," Johnny said. "But this round is ours."

"Well, you'll find a couple of Markheims stored in the cabin," the man said. "Don't be afraid to use them."

Johnny grinned and clapped the man on the shoulder. "Doubt if we'll need them at all," he said. But when he joined the twins on the ramp, he wasn't smiling any longer. "I don't like it," he said. "I was certain they'd have *somebody* snoopin' around."

"Maybe we're lucky," Greg said.

"Maybe." Johnny didn't sound convinced.

Inside the ship Tom and Johnny strapped down while Greg made his final check-down on the engines, gyros and wiring. The cabin was a tiny vault, with none of the spacious "living room" of the orbit ships. Tom leaned back in the acceleration cot, and listened to the count-down signals that came at one-minute intervals now. In the earphones he could hear the sporadic chatter between Greg and the control tower. No hint that this was anything but a routine blast-off.

But there was trouble ahead, Tom was certain of that. Everybody on Mars was aware that Roger Hunter's sons were heading out to the belt to pick up where he had left off. Greg had secured a leave of absence from Project Star-Jump, unwillingly granted, even though his part in their program had already been disrupted. Even they had heard the rumors that were adrift.

And if there was trouble now, they were on their own. The Asteroid Belt was a wilderness, untracked and unexplored, and except for an almost insignificant fraction, completely unknown. If there was trouble out there, there would be no one to help.

Somewhere below, the engines roared, and Tom felt the

weight on his chest, sudden and breathtaking. In the view screen the Martian horizon began to widen below them as the little ship rose into the dark sky.

They were on their way.

## Chapter Four

---

## "BETWEEN MARS AND JUPITER...."

AFTER all the tension of preparing for it, the trip out seemed interminable.

They were all impatient to reach their destination. During blast-off and acceleration they had watched Mars dwindle to a tiny red dot; then time seemed to stop altogether, and there was nothing to do but wait.

For the first eight hours of free-fall, after the engines had cut out, Tom was violently ill. He fought it desperately, gulping the pills Johnny offered and trying to keep them down. Gradually the waves of nausea subsided, but it was a full twenty-four hours before Tom felt like stirring from his cot to take up the shipboard routine.

And then there was nothing for him to do. Greg handled the navigation skillfully, while Johnny kept radio contact and busied himself in the storeroom, so Tom spent hours at the view screen. On the second day he spotted a tiny chunk of rock that was unquestionably an asteroid moving swiftly toward them. It passed at a tangent ten thousand miles ahead of them, and Greg started work at the computer, feeding in the data tapes that would ultimately guide the ship to its goal.

Pinpointing a given spot in the Asteroid Belt was a Gargantuan task, virtually impossible without the aid of the ship's computer to calculate orbits, speeds, and distances. Tom spent more and more time at the view screen, searching the blackness of space for more asteroid sightings. But except for an occasional tiny bit of debris hurtling by, he saw nothing but the changeless panorama of stars.

Johnny Coombs found him there on the third day, and laughed at his sour expression. "Gettin' impatient?"

"Just wondering when we'll reach the belt, is all," Tom said.

Johnny chuckled. "Hope you're not holdin' your breath. We've already been in the belt for the last forty-eight hours."

"Then where are all the asteroids?" Tom asked.

"Oh, they're here. You just won't see many of them. People always think there ought to be dozens of them around, like sheep on a hillside, but it doesn't work that way." Johnny peered at the screen. "Of course, to an astronomer the belt is loaded ... hundreds of thousands of chunks, all sizes from five hundred miles in diameter on down. But actually, those chunks are all tens of thousands of miles apart, and the belt *looks* just as empty as the space between Mars and Earth."

"Well, I don't see how we're ever going to find one particular rock," Tom said, watching the screen gloomily.

"It's not too hard. Every asteroid has its own orbit around the sun, and every one that's been registered as a claim has the orbit charted. The one we want isn't where it was when your dad's body was found ... it's been traveling in its orbit ever since. But by figuring in the fourth dimension, we can locate it."

Tom blinked. "Fourth dimension?"

"Time," Johnny Coombs said. "If we used only the three linear dimensions—length, width and depth—we'd end up at the place where the asteroid *was*, but that wouldn't help us much because it's been moving in its orbit ever since the patrol ship last pinpointed it. So we figure in a fourth dimension—the time that's passed since it was last spotted—and we can chart a collision course with it, figure out just where *we'll* have to be to meet it."

It was the first time that the idea of time as a "dimension" had ever made sense to Tom. They talked some more, until Johnny started bringing in fifth and sixth dimensions, and problems of irrational space and hyperspace, and got even himself confused.

"Anyway," Tom said, "I'm glad we've got a computer aboard."

"And a navigator," Johnny added. "Don't sell your brother short."

"Fat chance of that. Greg would never stand for it."

Johnny frowned. "You lads don't like each other very much, do you?" he said.

Tom was silent for a moment. Then he looked away. "We get along, I guess."

"Maybe. But sometimes just gettin' along isn't enough. Especially when there's trouble. Give it a thought, when you've got a minute or two."

Later, the three of them went over the computer results together. Johnny and Greg fed the navigation data into the ship's drive mechanism, checking and re-checking speeds and inclination angles. Already the Dutchman's orbital speed was matching the speed of Roger Hunter's asteroid, but the orbit had to be tracked so that they would arrive at the exact point in space to make contact. Tom was assigned to the view screen, and the long wait began.

He spotted their destination point an hour before the computer had predicted contact. At first a tiny pinpoint of reflected light in the scope, it gradually resolved into two pinpoints, and then three, in a tiny cluster. Greg cut in the rear and lateral jets momentarily, stabilizing their contact course. The dots grew larger.

Ten minutes later, Tom could see their goal clearly in the view screen—the place where Roger Hunter had died.

It was neither large nor small for an asteroid, an irregular chunk of rock and metal, perhaps five miles in diameter, lighted only by the dull reddish glow from the dime-sized sun. Like many such jagged chunks of debris that sprinkled the belt, this asteroid did not spin on any axis, but constantly presented the same face to the sun.

Just off the bright side the orbit ship floated, stable in its orbit next to the big rock, but so small in comparison that it looked like a tiny glittering toy balloon. Clamped in its rack on the orbit ship's side, airlock to airlock, was the *Scavenger*, the little scout ship that Roger Hunter had brought out from Mars on his last journey.

While Greg maneuvered the Dutchman into the empty landing rack below the *Scavenger* on the hull of the orbit ship, Johnny scanned the blackness around them through the viewscope, a frown wrinkling his forehead.

"Do you see anybody?" Tom asked.

"Not a sign. But I'm really lookin' for other rocks. I can see three that aren't too far away, but none has claim marks. This must have been the only one Roger was workin'."

"Claim marks?" Tom said.

Johnny pointed to the white markings on the surface of the rock below. "Chalk," he said. "It shows up almost before the rock does, and it gets down into the crevices in the rock, so that it's hard to erase. Discourages claim jumpin'. That's your dad's mark down there, and whatever he found must be down there too."

They stared at the ragged surface of the planetoid. Raw veins of metallic ore cut through it with streaks of color, but most of the sun side showed only the dull gray of iron and granite. There was nothing unusual about the surface that Tom could see.

"Could there be anything on the dark side?"

"Could be," Johnny said. "We'll have to go over it foot by foot. But first, we should go through the orbit ship and the *Scavenger*. If the patrol ship missed anything, we want to know it."

They waited until Greg had thrown out the magnetic cables to secure the Dutchman to the orbit ship's hull. Then Johnny checked the airlock, and they slipped into the light-weight pressure suits. He handed each of the twins one of the heavy Markheim stunners. "Make sure the safeties are on," he warned.

Tom fingered the safety dial and pushed the weapon into a storage slot in the suit. It took a direct hit from a stunner to paralyze a man, but the sub-sonics from an accidental discharge could be dangerous. He checked the leather case at his belt, with his father's revolver inside, and then followed Greg and Johnny through the airlock into the orbit ship.

At first they noticed nothing wrong. The ship was dark. It spun slowly on its axis, giving them just enough weight so they would not float free whenever they moved. Their boots clanged on the metal decks as they climbed up the curving corridor toward the control cabin.

Then Johnny threw a light switch, and they stared around them in amazement.

The cabin was a shambles. Everything that was not bolted down had been ripped open and thrown aside. Cabinet doors hung gaping, the contents spilled out in heaps onto the deck. A safe hung open on one hinge, the metal door twisted, obviously opened with an explosive charge. Even the metal plates housing the computer had been torn loose, exposing the banks of tubes and colored twists of wire.

Greg whistled through his teeth. "The major said the patrol crew had gone through the ship, but he didn't say they'd wrecked it."

"They didn't," Johnny said grimly. "No patrol ship would ever do this. Somebody else has been here since." He turned to the control panel, flipped switches, checked gauges. "Hydroponics are all right. Atmosphere's still good, we can take off these helmets. Fuel looks all right, storage holds—" He shook his head. "They weren't just looting, they were looking for something, all right. Let's look around and see if they missed anythin'."

It took them an hour to survey the wreckage. Not a compartment had been missed. Even the mattresses on the acceleration cots had been torn open, the spring stuffing tossed about helter-skelter. Tom went through the lock into the *Scavenger*. The scout ship too had been searched, rapidly but thoroughly.

But there was no sign of anything that Roger Hunter might have found.

Back in the control cabin Johnny was checking the ship's log. The old entries were on microfilm, stored on their spools near the reader. More recent entries were still recorded on tape. From the jumbled order, there was no doubt that the marauders had examined them. Johnny ran through them nevertheless, but there was nothing of interest. Routine navigational data; a record of the time of contact with the asteroid; a log of preliminary observations on the rock; nothing more. The last tape recorded the call-schedule Roger Hunter had set up with the patrol, a routine precaution used by all miners, to bring help if for some reason they should fail to check in on schedule.

There was no hint in the log of any extraordinary discovery.

"Are any tapes missing?" Greg wanted to know.

"Doesn't look like it. There's one here for each day period."

"I wonder," Tom said. "Dad always kept a personal log. You know, a sort of a diary, on microfilm." He peered into the film storage bin, checked through the spools. Then, from down beneath the last row of spools he pulled out a slightly smaller spool. "Here's something our friends missed, I bet."

It was not really a diary, just a sequence of notes, calculations and ideas that Roger Hunter had jotted down and microfilmed from time to time. The entries on the one spool went back for several years. Tom fed the spool into the reader, and they stared eagerly at the last few entries.

A series of calculations covering several pages, but with no notes to indicate what, exactly, Roger Hunter had been calculating. "Looks like he was plotting an orbit," Greg said. "But what orbit? And why? Nothing here to tell."

"It must have been important, though, or Dad wouldn't have filmed the pages," Tom said. "Anything else?"

Another sheet with more calculations. Then a short paragraph written in Roger Hunter's hurried scrawl. "No doubt now what it is," the words said. "Wish Johnny were here, show him a *real* bonanza, but he'll know soon enough if. . . ."

They stared at the scribbled, uncompleted sentence. Then Johnny Coombs let out a whoop. "I told you he found something! And he found it *here*, not somewhere else."

"Hold it," Greg said, peering at the film reader. "There's something more on the last page, but I can't read it."

Tom blinked at the entry. " '*Inter Jovem et Martem planetam interposui*,' " he read. He scratched his head. "That's Latin, and it's famous, too. Kepler wrote it, back before the asteroids were discovered. 'Between Jupiter and Mars I will put a planet.' "

Greg and Johnny looked at each other. "I don't get it," Greg said.

"Dad told me about that once," Tom said. "Kepler couldn't understand the long jump between Mars and Jupiter, when Venus and Earth and Mars were so close together. He figured there ought to be a planet out here—and he was right, in a way. There wasn't any one planet, unless you'd call Ceres a planet, but it wasn't just empty space between Mars and Jupiter, either. The asteroids were here."

"But why would Dad be writing that down?" Greg asked. "And what has it got to do with what he found?" He snapped off the reader switch angrily. "I don't understand any of this, and I don't like it. If Dad found something out here, where is it? And who tore this ship apart after the patrol ship left?"

"Probably the same ones that caused the 'accident' in the first place," Johnny said.

"But why did they come back?" Greg protested. "If they killed Dad, they must have known what he'd found before they killed him."

"You'd think so," Johnny conceded.

"Then why take the risk of coming back here again?"

"Maybe they *didn't* know," Tom said thoughtfully.

"What do you mean?"

"I mean maybe they killed him too soon. Maybe they thought they knew what he'd found and where it was, and then found out that they didn't, after all. Maybe Dad hid it."

Johnny Coombs shook his head. "No way a man can hide an ore strike."

"But suppose Dad did, somehow, and whoever killed him couldn't find it? It would be too late to make him tell then. They'd *have* to come back and look again, wouldn't they? And from the way they went about it, it looks as though they weren't having much luck."

"Then whatever Dad found would still be here, somewhere," Greg said.

"That's right."

"But where? There's nothing on this ship."

"Maybe not," Tom said, "but I'd like to take a look at that asteroid before we give up."

They paused in the big ore-loading lock to reclamp their pressure suit helmets, and looked down at the jagged chunk of rock a hundred yards below them. In the lock they found scooters, the little one-man propulsion units so commonly used for short-distance work in space, but decided not to use them. "They're clumsy," Johnny said, "and the bumper units in your suits will do just as well for this distance." He looked down at the rock. "I'll take the center section. You each take an edge and work in. Look for any signs of work on the surface—chisel marks, Murexide charges, anythin'."

"What about the dark side?" Greg asked.

"If we want to see anythin' there, we'll either have to rig lights or turn the rock around," Johnny said. "Let's cover this side first and see what we come up with."

He turned and leaped from the airlock, moving gracefully down toward the surface, using the bumper unit to guide himself, with short bursts of compressed $CO_2$ from the nozzle. Greg followed, pushing off harder and passing Johnny halfway down. Tom hesitated. It looked easy enough, but he remembered the violent nausea of his first few hours of freefall.

Finally he gritted his teeth and jumped off after Greg. Instantly he knew that he had jumped too hard. He shot away from the orbit ship like a bullet. The jagged asteroid surface leaped up at him. Frantically he grabbed for the bumper nozzle and pulled the trigger, trying to break his fall.

He felt the nozzle jerk in his hand, and then, abruptly, he was spinning off at a wild tangent from the asteroid, head over heels. For a moment it seemed that asteroid, orbit ship and stars were all wheeling crazily around him. Then he realized what had happened. He fired the bumper again, and went spinning twice as fast. The third time he timed the blast, aiming the nozzle carefully, and the spinning almost stopped.

He fought down nausea, trying to get his bearings. He was three hundred yards out from the asteroid, almost twice as far from the orbit ship. He stared down at the rock as he moved slowly away from it. Before, from the orbit ship, he had been able to see only the bright side of the huge rock; now he could see the sharp line of darkness across one side.

But there was something else. . . .

He fired the bumper again to steady himself, peering into the blackness beyond the light line on the rock. He snapped on his helmet lamp, aimed the spotlight beam down to the dark rock surface. Greg and Johnny were landing now on the bright side, with Greg almost out of sight over the 'horizon', but Tom's attention was focused on something he could see only now as he moved away from the asteroid surface.

His spotlight caught it—something bright and metallic, completely hidden on the dark side, lying in close to the surface but not quite on the surface. Suddenly Tom knew what it was—the braking jets of a Class I Ranger, crouching beyond the reach of sunlight in the shadow of the asteroid.

Swiftly he fired the bumper again, turning back toward the orbit ship. His hand went to the speaker switch, but he caught himself in time. Any warning shouted to Greg and Johnny would certainly be picked up by the ship. But he had to give warning somehow.

He tumbled into the airlock, searching for a flare in his web belt. It was a risk—the ranger ship might pick up the flash—but he had to take it. He was unscrewing the fuse cap from the flare when he saw Greg and Johnny leap up from the asteroid surface.

Then he saw what had alarmed them. Slowly, the ranger was moving out from its hiding place behind the rock. Tom reached out to catch Greg as he came plummeting into the lock. There was a flash from the ranger's side, and Johnny Coombs' voice boomed in his earphones: "Get inside! Get the lock closed, fast."

Johnny caught the lip of the lock, dragged himself inside frantically. They were spinning the airlock door closed when they heard the thundering explosion, felt the ship lurch under their feet, and all three of them went crashing to the deck.

## Chapter Five

---

## THE BLACK RAIDER

FOR a stunned moment they were helpless as they struggled to pick themselves up. The stable airlock deck was suddenly no longer stable. It was lurching back and forth like a rowboat on a heavy sea. They grabbed the shock bars along the bulkheads to steady themselves. "What happened?" Greg yelped. "I saw a ship—"

As if in answer there was another crash below decks, and the lurching became worse. "They're firin' on us, that's what happened," Johnny Coombs growled.

"Well, they're shaking us loose at the seams," Greg said. "We've got to get this crate out of here." He reached for his helmet and began unsnapping his pressure suit.

"Leave it on," Johnny snapped.

"But we can't move fast enough in these things."

"Leave it on all the same. If they split the hull open, you'll be dead in ten seconds without a suit."

Somewhere below they heard the steady *clang-clang-clang* of the emergency stations bell. Already one of the compartments somewhere had been breached and was pouring its air out into the vacuum of space. "But what can we do?" Greg cried. "They could tear us apart!"

"First, we see what they've already done," Johnny said, spinning the wheel on the inner lock. "If they plan to tear us apart, we're done for, but they may want to try to board us."

The lock came open, and they started down the corridor, lurching helplessly with the ship, crashing back and forth into the bulkheads as they ran. The alarm bell continued its urgent clanging. Somewhere above they heard the wrenching grate of tortured metal as a seam gave way.

Like all orbit ships, this one had been built in space, in the form of a sphere that was never intended to enter the powerful gravitational field or the thick atmosphere of any planet. Orbit ships were the work horses of space; their engines were built for friction-free maneuverability, and their spherical design provided the most storage space for the least surface area. Once placed in a desired orbit, such a ship would travel like any planetoid in its own ellipse around the sun.

For passenger and freight traffic between the planets, orbit ships were reliable and cheap. As headquarters bases for asteroid mining, they were perfect. But an orbit ship was never designed for combat. Its hull was a thin layer of aluminum alloy, held in shape by the great pressure of the artificial atmosphere inside it. It had maneuverability, but no speed. And its size—huge in comparison to the scout ships that used it for a base—made it a perfect target.

An orbit ship under fire was completely vulnerable. One well-placed shell could rip it open like a balloon.

Tom and Greg followed Johnny up the corridor between the storage holds of the outer layer, and lurched down a ladder to the middle layer where the control cabin was located. In control they found alarm lights flashing in three places on the instrument panel. Another muffled crash roared through the ship, and a new row of lights sprang on along the panel.

"How are the engines?" Greg asked, staring at the flickering lights.

"Can't tell. Looks like they're firing at the main jets, but they've ripped open three storage holds, too. They're trying to disable us."

"What about the *Scavenger?*"

Johnny checked a gauge. "The airlock compartment is all right, so the scout ships haven't been touched. They couldn't fire on them without splittin' the whole ship down the middle." He leaned forward, flipped on the view screen, and an image came into focus.

It was a Class I Ranger, and there was no doubt of its origin. Like the one they had seen berthing at the Sun Lake City racks, this ship had a glossy black hull, with the golden triangle-and-J insignia standing out in sharp relief in the dim sunlight.

"It's our friends, all right," Johnny said.

"But what are they trying to do?" Tom said.

Even as they watched, a pair of scooters broke from the side of the Ranger and slid down toward the sun side of the asteroid. "I don't know," Johnny said. "I think they intended to stay hidden, until Tom lost control of his bumper and got far enough around there to spot them." He frowned as the first scooter touched down on the asteroid surface.

"Can't we fire on them?" Greg said angrily.

"Not the way this tub is lurching around. They've got our main gyros, and the auxiliaries aren't powerful enough to steady us. Another blast or two could send us spinnin' like a top, and we'd have nothing to stabilize us."

There was another flash from the Ranger's hull, and the ship jerked under their feet. "Well, we're a sitting duck here," Greg said. "Maybe those engines will still work." He slid into the control seat, flipped the drive switches to fire the side jets in opposite pairs. They fired, steadying the lurching of the ship somewhat, but there was no response from the main engines. "No good. We couldn't begin to run from them."

"They could outrun us anyway," Tom said, watching the view screen. "And they're moving in closer now."

It was true. The black ship, which had been lying out several miles from them, was now looming larger. As they watched, the Ranger maneuvered toward the #3 landing rack, just above the rack that held the *Scavenger*.

"They're going to board us," Tom cried.

Johnny nodded, his eyes suddenly bright. "I think you're right. And if they do, we may have a chance. But we've got to split up. Greg, you take the control cabin here; try to keep them out if you can. Tom, you cover the main corridor to the storage holds. I'll take the engine-room section. That will sew up the entrances to control, here, and give us a chance to stop them."

"They may have a dozen men," Tom said. "They could just shoot us down."

"I don't think so," Johnny said. "They want *us*, not the ship, or they wouldn't bother to board us. We may not be able to hold them off, but we can try."

"What about making a run for it in the *Scavenger?*" Greg said.

Johnny chuckled grimly. "It'd be a mighty short run. That

Ranger's got homing shells that could blow the *Scavenger* to splinters if we tried it. Our best bet is to put up such a brawl that they'll think twice about takin' us."

The Ranger had come in very close now. Magnetic grappling cables shot out from the dark hull, clanging on the steel plates above and below #3 rack. Slowly the ship began pulling itself in to the orbit ship's side.

And then the two scooters shot up from the asteroid surface, heading for the loading lock. Johnny looked at Tom. "Let's go, and don't be afraid to hit them."

They parted in the corridor outside control, Johnny heading down for the engine-room corridor, while Tom ran up toward the main outer-shell corridor, Markheim stunner in his hand. The entire outer shell of the ship was storage space, each compartment separately sealed and connected with the two main corridors that circled the ship. On each side these corridors came together to join the short entry corridors from the scout ship's airlocks.

Tom knew that the only way the ship could be boarded was through those locks. A man stationed at the place where the main corridors joined could block any entry from the locks, as long as he could hold his position. He reached the junction of the corridors, and crouched close to the wall. By peering around the corner, he had a good view of the airlock corridor. He waited until his heart stopped pounding in his ears. Then he heard the clanging sound of boots on metal and the sucking noise of the airlock in operation.

They were aboard.

Tom gripped the Markheim tightly and dialed it down to a narrow beam. Nobody had ever been killed by a stunner, but a direct hit with a narrow beam could paralyze a man for three days. He would have to hit his target with no help from the sub-sonic reflections, but he knew that whoever he hit wouldn't go any farther.

There was movement at the far end of the airlock corridor. A helmeted head peered around the turn in the corridor; then two men in pressure suits moved into view, walking cautiously, weapons in hand. Tom shrank back against the wall, certain they had not seen him. He waited until they were almost to the junction with the main corridor; then he took aim and pressed the trigger stud on his Markheim. There was an ugly ripping sound as the gun jerked in his hand. The two men dropped as though they had been poleaxed.

A shout, a scrape of metal against metal, and a shot ripped back at him from the end of the corridor. Tom jerked back fast, but not quite fast enough. He felt a sledge-hammer blow on his shoulder, felt his arm jerk in a cramping spasm while the corridor echoed the low rumble of sub-sonics. He flexed his arm to work out the spasm. They were using a wide beam, hardly strong enough to stun a man. His heart pounded. They were being careful, very careful.

Two more men rounded the bend in the corridor. Tom fired, but they hit the deck fast, and the beam missed. The first one jerked to his feet, charged up the corridor toward him, dodging and sliding. Tom followed him in his sights, fired three times as the Markheim heated up in his hand. The beam hit the man's leg, dumping him to the deck, and bounced off to catch the second one.

But now there was another sound coming from the corridor behind him. Voices, shouts, clanging of boots. He pressed against the wall, listening. The sounds were from below—probably the men on the scooters. They must have gotten past Johnny. Tom looked around helplessly. If they came up behind him, he was trapped in a crossfire. But if he left his position, more men could come in through the airlock. Even now two more came around the bend, starting up the corridor for him.

Quite suddenly, the lights went out.

The men stopped. Sound stopped. The corridor was pitch black. Tom fired wildly down the corridor, heard shouts and oaths from the men, but he could see nothing; then, ahead, a flicker of light as a head lamp went on. The men from the airlock were close, moving in on him, and from behind he saw light bouncing off the corridor walls.

He jerked open the hatch to a storage hold, ducked inside, and slammed the hatch behind him. He pressed against the wall, panting. Silence, blackness, a close, stuffy smell. . . .

He waited.

Footsteps clanged by, muffled voices came to him faintly. Tom felt his way deeper into the compartment and ducked behind some storage crates. Here concealment was possible; they would find him, but only after a search. Meanwhile, he could wait and hide, perhaps catch them from the rear.

The hopelessness of the situation struck him like a black wave. Three determined men could hold off the raiders for a while, but not for long. The raiders would succeed by weight of numbers, if for no other reason. An orbit ship was simply not built for fighting. There were no good strategic points from which to defend it.

Ultimately, the Jupiter Equilateral ship would take them and the very best they could do was make the capture a little more difficult for the raiders. In the long run, it wouldn't make any difference, they would still be captured.

An idea flickered in Tom's mind.

It was a chance . . . a long chance . . . but it was something.

If they were going to be captured in spite of anything they could do, even a long chance was worth trying.

He waited in the darkness and tried to think it through. It was a wild idea, an utterly impossible idea, he had never heard of it being tried before, but *any* chance was better than none. He remembered what Johnny had said in the control cabin. The ranger ship would have homing shells. An attempt to make a run with the *Scavenger* might be disastrous.

He thought about it, trying to reason it out. The Jupiter Equilateral men obviously wanted them alive. A single shell could have split the orbit ship open at the seams, but the Ranger was taking the more dangerous choice of boarding them. That could only mean that at least one of them was to be taken alive.

But why?

*Because they knew something that Jupiter Equilateral didn't know,* or Jupiter Equilateral thought they did.

The answer stared him in the face. Jupiter Equilateral had found out about Roger Hunter's bonanza. They had killed him in order to get it, but they had killed him too soon. They had searched the orbit ship and the asteroid for the big strike they knew was there.

*But they hadn't found it.*

And now they did not dare to kill Roger Hunter's sons, because he might have told them where the bonanza was.

Tom grinned fiercely in the darkness. It was the answer, nothing else made sense. It meant that the men on the Ranger would have orders to pick up the three of them and bring them back to the Ranger's orbit ship as quickly as possible. If they had the secret, they must be taken alive.

But Jupiter Equilateral would not dare let any one of

them break away. If one of them got back to Mars, the whole U.N. patrol would be out in the belt.

The plan began to take shape.

Tom heard the storage room hatch swing open, saw head lamps flash across the piles of crates. There was a rumble of voices; he caught a few words.

". . . burned out the main switch completely. Take a month to repair it."

"Can't see anything with these lamps."

"He must have come in here, or the next one."

Tom could see the head lamps, but he held his fire. He might miss, and they would have him. He waited as they conferred, flashing the beams around the hold, then moved out into the corridor, leaving the hatchway open.

Tom continued to wait, motionless, for five minutes. The plan was clear in his mind, but he had to let Greg know. He fingered the control of his helmet radio. The boarding party would have a snooper, but if he was quick, they wouldn't have time to nail him. He buzzed an attention code. "Greg? Can you hear me?"

Silence. He buzzed again, and waited. What was wrong? Had they already broken through to the control cabin and taken Greg? He buzzed again. "Greg! Sound off if you can hear me."

More silence. Then a click. "Tom?"

"Here. Are you all right?"

"So far. You?"

"They got past me, but they didn't hit me. How's Johnny?"

"I don't know," Greg said. "I think he's been hurt. You'd better get off, they'll have snoopers."

"All right, listen," Tom said. "How does it look to you?"

"Bad. We're outnumbered, they'll be through to here any minute."

"All right, I've got an idea. It's risky, but it might let us pull something out of this mess. I'll need some time, though."

"How much?"

"Ten, fifteen minutes."

There was an edge to Greg's voice. "What are you planning?"

"I can't tell you, they're listening in. But if it works...."

"Look, don't do anything rash."

"I can't hear you," Tom said. "Try to hold them for fifteen minutes, and don't worry. Take care of yourself."

He snapped off the speaker and moved to the hatchway. The corridor was empty, and pitch black. He started down toward the airlock, then stopped short at the sound of voices and the flicker of head lamps up ahead. He crouched back, but the lights were not moving. Guards at the lock, making certain that nobody tried to board their own ship. Tom grinned to himself. They weren't missing any bets, he thought.

Except one. There was one bet they wouldn't even think of.

He backtracked to the storage hold, crossed through it, and out into the far corridor. He followed the gentle curve of the deck a quarter of the way around the ship. Twice along the way he stumbled in the darkness, but saw no sign of the raiders. At last he reached the far side, and the corridor leading to #2 airlock. Again he could see the lamps of the guards around the bend; they were stationed directly inside their own lock.

Inching forward, he peered into blackness. Each step made a muffled clang on the deck plates. He edged his boots along as quietly as possible, reaching along the wall with his hand until he felt the lip of a hatchway.

The lights and voices seemed nearer now. In the dim reflected light he saw the sign on the door of the hatchway:

#2 Airlock

BE SURE PRESSURE GAUGE IS AT ZERO

BEFORE OPENING HATCH

He checked the gauge, silently spun the wheel. There was a *ping* as the seals broke. He pulled the hatch open just enough to squeeze into the lock, then closed it behind him. He switched on the pumps, waiting impatiently until the red "All Clear" signal flashed on. Then he opened the outside lock.

Just beyond, he could see the sleek silvery lines of the *Scavenger* with its airlock hanging open.

He hesitated for a moment. Once he started, there would be no chance to turn back. His plan might work, but it was a desperate chance, with incredible risks.

But he knew it was their only chance.

Tom took a deep breath and jumped across the gap to the open lock of the *Scavenger*.

## Chapter Six

## THE LAST RUN OF THE *SCAVENGER*

TO Greg Hunter the siege of the orbit ship had been a nerve-wracking game of listening and waiting for something to happen.

In the darkness of the control cabin he stretched his fingers, cramped from gripping the heavy Markheim stunner, and checked the corridor outside again. There was no sound in the darkness there, no sign of movement. Somewhere far below he heard metal banging on metal; minutes before he thought he had heard the sharp ripping sound of a stunner blast overhead, but he wasn't sure. Wherever the fighting was going on, it was not here.

He shook his head as his uneasiness mounted. Why hadn't Johnny come back? Why was there no sign of the marauders in the control cabin corridor? This should have been the first place they would head for, if they planned to take the ship, but there had been nothing but silence and darkness.

Unless they were after something entirely different. . . .

He checked his stunner for the tenth time, tightened down

the beam. He knew his position was good. The control cabin was the main compartment on the middle level of the ship. All corridors converged on two main control room corridors, front and rear. Greg had laboriously barricaded the rear entrance until nothing smaller than a bulldozer could push through. Anyone heading for the control cabin would have to come by the front corridor.

And that, Greg thought grimly, might be a very costly operation.

All the same, he wished that Johnny hadn't left. The big miner had made his way to the control cabin just a few minutes after the boarding party had landed, his left arm hanging uselessly at his side, right hand gripping his stunner. "Winged me," he had said angrily. "The two on scooters came in the lock just behind me and jumped me. I stopped one of them, but the other broke away and headed this way."

"He didn't come in here," Greg said.

"Well, it won't be long before somebody does," Johnny said. "It looks bad. Must be two dozen of them aboard. We can't hope to hold out very long."

"We've got to," Greg said. "If they get to us, we're done for."

"I'm not so sure about that," Johnny said thoughtfully. "Those boys had a perfect shot at me, but they used wide beams. Seems to me they're being awful careful, for pirates."

"What for?"

"I think they want us in good shape. Maybe Tom is right, maybe they couldn't find your dad's strike, and think we know where it is."

"Maybe so," Greg admitted, "but this is piracy just the same, and that means they'll never dare let us get back to

Mars, any of us." He turned to Johnny. "Can't we do anything to even the odds a little?"

"If we could manage to disable the Ranger ship, it might help."

"But they'll be guarding it."

"True, but it's worth a try. Can you hold the gate here?"

"I can try."

"All right. I'll be back." Johnny had checked the power pack in his stunner and then vanished into the gloom of the corridor. Now, after fifteen minutes, there was no sign of him, nothing but darkness and oppressive, ominous silence.

Greg waited. Suddenly, bitterly, he realized the hopelessness of their situation. Even if Johnny did manage to damage the Ranger ship, what difference would it make? The three of them had been fools to come out here, idiots to ignore Tawney's warning. Hadn't Tawney told them in so many words that there would be trouble? But they had come out anyway, just begging for it.

Well, now they had what they'd begged for. Greg slammed his fist into his palm angrily. What had they expected? That the big company would step aside for them, with a fortune hanging in the balance? If they had even begun to think it through before they started. . . .

But they hadn't, and now it was too late. They were under attack. Johnny was off on a fool's errand, gone too long for comfort, and Tom—Greg glanced at his watch. It had been ten minutes since Tom's call. What had he meant? A plan, he said. A long chance.

Greg checked the corridor again, listening for any sound. What Tom did was none of his business. He hadn't wanted his brother to come along in the first place. If Tom got himself into a jam now, there was nothing *he* could do about it.

But he couldn't shake off the cold feeling in his chest when he thought about Tom. If something happened to him, then what? The cold feeling deepened into an ache.

Once, long ago, he and Tom had been inseparable. He remembered those days with sudden vivid clearness. They had gone everywhere and done everything together. They'd actually been *friends*. But things had been different then. Dad had been working in the city then, and Mom had been alive, and things had been different.

And then the sickness had come, and torn everything apart. A native Martian virus, the doctor had said, a neurotoxic virus like the old Earth-side polio, only worse. First it hit Mom, then Tom, striking without warning.

He remembered the horrible, endless night he had waited at the infirmary with Dad, until the doctor came out and told them that Mom was gone, that there was only a slender chance for Tom. He remembered Dad's gray face that night. It was weeks before they were sure that Tom was going to live, months before he was back on his feet, pale and weak, a ghost of his twin brother. It had been everything for Tom in those days, *everything* for Tom. The sickness hadn't even touched Greg. By the time Tom was well again, Greg was two years ahead in school, bigger than Tom, stronger than Tom, and somehow they weren't friends any more.

Until now, when something stronger than either of them drew them together again. Greg fought down the bitter memories, and wished suddenly that the cold ache in his chest would go away, that Tom would appear down the corridor.

A sound jerked him out of his reverie. He tensed, gripping the stunner, peering into the darkness. Had he heard something? Or, was it his own foot scraping on the deck plate? He held his breath, listening, and the sound came again, louder.

Someone was moving stealthily up the corridor.

Greg waited, covered by the edge of the hatchway. It might be Johnny returning, or maybe even Tom, but there was no sign of recognition. Whoever it was was coming silently. . . .

A beam of light flared from a head lamp, and he saw the blue crackle of a stunner. He jerked back as the beam bounced off the metal walls. Then he was firing point-blank down the corridor, his stunner on a tight beam, a deadly pencil of violent energy. He heard a muffled scream as a bulk loomed up in front of him and crashed to the deck at his feet.

He fired again. Another crash, a shout, and the sound of footsteps, retreating. He waited, his heart pounding, but there was nothing more.

The first attempt on the control cabin had failed.

Five minutes later the second attempt began. This time there was no warning sound. A sudden, ear-splitting crash, a groan of tortured metal, and the barricaded hatchway glowed dull red. Another crash followed. The edge of the hatch split open, pouring acrid Murexide fumes into the cabin. A third explosion breached the door six inches; Greg could see head lamps in the corridor beyond.

He fired through the crack, pressing down the stud until the stunner scorched his hand. Then he heard boots clanging up the other corridor. He pressed back against the wall, waited until the sounds were near, then threw open the hatch. For an instant he made a perfect target, but the raiders did not fire. The stunner buzzed in his hand, and once again the footfalls retreated.

They *were* being careful!

Silence then, and blackness. Minutes passed ... five, ten ... Greg checked the time again. It was over twenty minutes since Tom had talked to him. What had happened? Whatever Tom had planned must have misfired, or something would have happened by now. For a moment he considered leaving his post and starting down the dark corridor to search, but to search where? There was nothing to do but wait and hope for a miracle.

Suddenly the lights blazed on in the control cabin and the corridor outside. An attention signal buzzed in Greg's earphones. "All right, Hunter, it's all over," a voice grated. "You've got five minutes to get down to #3 lock. If you make us come and get you, you'll get hurt."

"I'll chance it," Greg snapped back. "Come on up."

"We're through fooling," the voice said. "You'd better get down here. And bring your brother with you."

"Sure," Greg said. "Start holding your breath."

The contact broke for a moment, then clicked on again. This time it was another voice. "We've got Johnny Coombs down here," it said. "You want him to stay alive, you start moving. Without your stunner."

Greg chewed his lip. They could be bluffing, but they might not be. "I want to see Johnny," he said.

On the control panel a view screen flickered to life. "Take a look," the voice said in his earphones.

They had Johnny, all right. A burly guard was holding his good arm behind his back. Greg could see the speaker wires jerked loose from his helmet.

"It's up to you," the voice said. "You've got three minutes. If you're not down here by then, this helmet comes off and your friend goes out the lock. It's quick that way, but it's not very pleasant."

Johnny was shaking his head violently. The guard wrenched at his arm, and the miner's face twisted in pain. "Two minutes," the voice said.

"Okay," Greg said. "I'm coming down."

"Drop the stunner right there."

He dropped the weapon onto the deck. Three steps out into the corridor, and two guards were there to meet him, stunners raised. They marched him up the ramp to the outer level corridor and around to #3 lock.

They were waiting there with Johnny. A moment later the guards herded them through the lock and into the hold of the Ranger ship, stripped off their suits, and searched them.

A big man with a heavy face and coarse black hair came into the cabin. He looked at Johnny and Greg and grunted. "You must be Hunter," he said to Greg. "Where's the other one?"

"What other one?" Greg said.

"Your brother. Where is he?"

"How would I know?"

The man's face darkened. "You'd be smart to watch your tongue," he said. "We know there were three of you, we want the other one."

"I told you I don't know where he is," Greg said.

The man turned to a guard. "What about it?"

"Don't know, Doc. Nobody's reported him."

"Then take a crew and search the ship. We were due back hours ago. He's in there somewhere."

"Sure, Doc." The guard disappeared through the lock. The man called Doc motioned Greg and Johnny through into the main cabin.

The Ranger was large and luxurious, with modern instruments, a large colloid computer, and a view screen that picked up 210 degrees in a single panel. The screen was on. Greg could see the silvery curve of the orbit ship alongside, with a gaping hole torn through into the main storage hold. Below, the bright side of the asteroid was visible. He could see the pockmarked hull of the *Scavenger* clinging to its rack just below them.

"What are you planning to do with us?" he demanded.

"You'll find out soon enough." Doc's mouth twisted angrily. "You're important people, didn't you know that? Kid gloves they told us to use. So now I've got nine stun-shocked men, and you haven't even been scratched." He threw his suit in the corner. "You ever been stun-shocked?"

"No."

"Well, it's lots of fun. Maybe when Tawney gets through with you we'll have a chance to show you how much fun it is."

A guard burst into the cabin. "Doc, there's nobody there! We've scoured the ship."

"You think he just floated away in his space suit?" Doc growled. "*Find him.* Tawney only needs one of them, but we can't take a chance on the other one getting back—" He broke off, his eyes on the view screen. "Did you check those scout ships?"

"No, I thought—"

"Get down there and check them." Doc turned back to the view screen impatiently.

Greg caught Johnny's eye, saw the big miner's worried frown. "Where is he?" he whispered.

"I don't know. Thought you did."

"All I know is he had some kind of scheme in mind."

"Shut up," Doc said to them. "If you're smart, you'll be strapping down before we—" He broke off in midsentence, listening.

Suddenly, the Ranger ship had begun to vibrate. Somewhere, far away, there was the muffled rumble of engines.

Doc whirled to the view screen. Greg and Johnny looked at the same instant, and Johnny groaned.

Below them, the *Scavenger's* jets were flaring. First the pale starter flame, then a long stream of fire, growing longer as the engines developed thrust.

Doc slammed down a switch, roared into the speaker. "That scout ship—stop it! He's trying to make a break!"

Two guards appeared at the lock almost instantly, but it was too late. Already she was straining at her magnetic cable moorings; then the exhaust flared, and the little scout ship leaped away from the orbit ship, moving out at a tangent to the asteroid's orbit, picking up speed, moving faster and faster. . . .

In toward the orbit of Mars.

Doc had gone pale. Now he snapped on the speaker again. "Frank? Stand by on missile control. He's asking for it."

"Right," a voice came back. "I'm sighting in."

The *Scavenger* was moving fast now, dwindling in the view screen. One panel of the screen went telescopic to track her. "All right," Doc said. "Fire one and two."

From both sides of the Ranger, tiny rockets flared. Like twin bullets the homing shells moved out, side by side, in the track of the escaping *Scavenger*. With a strangled cry, Greg leaped forward, but Johnny caught his arm.

"Johnny, *Tom's on that thing!*"

"I know. But he's got a chance."

Already the homing shells were out of sight; only the twin flares were visible. Greg stared helplessly at the tiny light spot of the *Scavenger*. At first she had been moving straight, but now she was dodging and twisting, her side jets flaring at irregular intervals. The twin pursuit shells mimicked each change in course, drawing closer to her every second.

There was a flash, so brilliant it nearly blinded them, and the *Scavenger* burst apart in space. The second shell struck a fragment; there was another flash. Then there was nothing but a nebulous powdering of tiny metal fragments.

The last run of the *Scavenger* had ended.

Dazed, Greg turned away from the screen, and somewhere, as if in a dream, he heard Doc saying, "All right, boys, strap this pair down. We've got a lot of work to do before we can get out of here."

# Chapter Seven

## PRISONERS

**W**HEREVER they were planning to take them, the captors took great pains to make sure that their prisoners did not escape before they were underway. Greg and Johnny were strapped down securely into acceleration cots. Two burly guards were assigned to them. The guards took their job seriously. One of them watched the captives at all times, and both held their stunners on ready.

Meanwhile, under Doc's orders, the crew of the Jupiter Equilateral ship began a systematic looting of the orbit ship they had disabled. Earlier they had merely searched the cabins and compartments. Now a steady stream of pressure suited men crossed through the airlocks into the crippled vessel and marched back with packing cases full of tape records, microfilm spools, stored computer data—anything that might conceivably contain information. The control cabin was literally torn apart. Every storage hold was ransacked.

A team of six men was dispatched to the asteroid surface,

searching for any sign of mining or prospecting activity. They came back an hour later, long-faced and empty-handed. Doc took their reports, his scowl growing deeper and deeper.

Finally the last of the searchers reported in. "Doc, we've scraped it clean, and there's nothing there. Not one thing that we didn't check before."

"There's *got* to be something there," Doc said.

"You tell me where else to look, and I'll do it."

Doc shook his head ominously. "Tawney's not going to like it," he said. "There's no other place it *could* be."

"Well, at least we have this pair," the other said, jerking a thumb at Greg and Johnny. "They'll know."

Doc looked at them darkly. "Yes, and they'll tell, too, or I don't know Tawney."

Greg watched all this happening. He heard the noises, saw the packing cases come through the cabin, and still he could not quite believe it. He had had nightmares, years before, when horrible things seemed to be happening around him without quite including him. Now this seemed like one of those nightmares. He kept telling himself that it wasn't true, that the thing he had seen happen to the *Scavenger* had not really happened at all. But unlike the others, this nightmare didn't go away. It was real, and this time he was part of it.

He and Johnny. He saw Johnny on the cot next to him, watching the busy crewmen with dull eyes, and he knew that it had hit Johnny as hard as it hit him. Except for the guards, the crewmen hardly noticed them; it was as though what had happened to the *Scavenger* was just part of the day's work to them, as though nothing out of the ordinary had happened at all. At one point Greg caught a few words, as a couple of men paused for a smoke; there was nothing but pleased satisfaction in their voices. "Frankie done a great job of shootin', huh?"

"Yeah! Can't beat those shells for close work. Just turn 'em loose, and whammo! Guy musta been crazy, tryin' to pull out like that."

Greg caught Johnny's eye, then turned away, suddenly sick. Johnny shook his head. "Take it easy, boy."

"He didn't even have a chance," Greg said.

"I know. He must have known too."

"But why? What was he thinking of?"

"Maybe he thought he could make it. Maybe he thought it was the only chance."

There was no other answer that Greg could see, and the ache in his chest cut deeper. A skillful pilot in a well-armed, powerful ship *might* have had a chance, at least a chance to try outrunning the shells. But Tom barely knew which switches to pull to start the engine running. Something deep in Greg's mind kept digging at him. *It was your fault,* the something seemed to say. *You let him come out here, you should never have let him leave Mars.*

He thrust the gnawing thought from his mind and tried to make himself worry about what might be waiting for them wherever they were going. Where *were* they going? Certainly not back to Mars. Probably to one of the Jupiter Equilateral orbit ships tending the mining rigs somewhere else in the belt. Somehow, he couldn't worry, he didn't even care what was going to happen, not any more.

First Dad, then Tom, and all because of something he didn't even know about, something he couldn't even guess. Whatever Dad had found, he had concealed it so well that nobody could find it. Dad had found a bonanza, and died for it.

But no bonanza in the world could bring Tom back. Nothing but a miracle could do that, and miracles didn't happen. Now, gradually, the shock was wearing off, and Greg felt a cold ball of anger growing in his throat.

There was no way to bring his brother back now. However things had been between them, they could never be changed now. But he knew that as long as he was still breathing, somebody, somehow, was going to answer for that last desperate run of the *Scavenger*.

He lay back in the couch, gripping the handgrips, waiting for the count-down to begin.

He didn't know that the miracle had already happened.

It had been an excellent idea, Tom Hunter thought to himself, and it had worked perfectly, exactly as he had planned it—so far. But now, as he clung to his precarious perch, he wondered if it had not worked out a little too well. The first flush of excitement that he had felt when he saw the *Scavenger* blow apart in space had begun to die down; on its heels came the unpleasant truth, the realization that only the easy part now lay behind him. The hard part was yet to come, and if that were to fail. . . .

He fought down panic, struggled to get a more comfortable position. Now, more than anything else, he wished that there had been some way to warn Greg and Johnny of what he intended to do.

But of course there had been no way to do that if the plan was to work. They weren't good enough actors; they would certainly give the show away if they suspected, even for a moment that Tom was still very much alive.

Now that the first part was over, he was committed. There could be no turning back, no reconsidering. The crew from the Ranger had done too good a job of wrecking the orbit ship and the Dutchman they had brought out from Mars. There was no alternative now but to follow through.

He realized, suddenly, that he was afraid. He was well enough concealed at the moment, clinging tightly against the outside hull of the Ranger ship, hidden behind the open airlock door. But soon the airlock would be pulled closed, and then the real test would come.

Carefully, he ran through the plan again in his mind. He was certain now that his reasoning was right. There had been two dozen men on the raider ship; there had been no question, even at the start, that they would succeed in boarding the orbit ship and taking its occupants prisoner. The Jupiter Equilateral ship had not appeared there by coincidence. Its occupants had come looking for something that they had not found.

And the only source of information left was Roger Hunter's sons. They with their friend, Johnny Coombs, might have held the ship for hours, or even days, but with engines and radios smashed, there had been no hope of contacting Mars for help. Ultimately, they would have been taken.

As he crouched in the dark storage hold of the orbit ship, Tom had realized this. He had also realized that, once captured, they would never have been freed and allowed to return to Mars. They would have been safe only until the Jupiter Equilateral men were convinced that they could not, or would not reveal where Roger Hunter had hidden his treasure. From that point on, they were dead; it would only be a matter of where, when, and how. Perhaps another "accident" like the "accident" that had happened to Dad. They would be found, sometime, somewhere, frozen corpses in space, and that would be the end of it.

It had been that line of thought, as he waited in the storage hold, that had led to his plan. If the three of them were taken, they were finished. But what if only two were taken? He had pushed it aside as a foolish idea, at first. The boarding party would never rest until they had accounted for all three. They wouldn't dare go back to their headquarters leaving one live man behind to tell the story. . . .

*Unless they thought the man was not alive!* If they could be sure of that—absolutely *certain* of it—they would not hesitate to take away the remaining two. And if, by chance, the third man wasn't as dead as they thought he was, and could find a way to follow them home, there might still be a chance to free the other two.

It was then that Tom thought of the *Scavenger* and knew that he had found a way.

In the cabin of the little scout ship he had worked swiftly, fearful that at any minute one of the maurauders might come aboard to search it. Tom was no rocket pilot, but he did know that the count-down was automatic, and that every ship could run on an autopilot, as a drone, following a prescribed course until it ran out of fuel. Even the shell evasion mechanism could be set on automatic.

Quickly he set the autopilot, plotted a simple high-school math course for the ship, a course the Ranger ship would be certain to see, and to fire upon. He set the count-down clock to give himself plenty of time for the next step—and stopped.

A flaw. He knew a moment of panic. What if somebody came aboard in the meantime and found the controls set? A simple flip of a switch, and the plan would be scuttled.

His mind raced to find a way around the problem. Both the airlock to the *Scavenger* and to the orbit ship worked on electric motors. The *Scavenger* was grappled to the orbit ship's hull by magnetic cables. Tom dug into the ship's repair locker, found the wires and fuses that he needed, and swiftly started to work.

It was an ingenious device, he decided, when he was finished, very simple, and almost fool-proof. The inner airlock door in the orbit ship was triggered to a fuse. He had left it ajar; the moment it was closed by anyone intending to board the *Scavenger,* the fuse would burn, a circuit would open, and the little ship's autopilot would go on active. The ship would blast away from its moorings, head out towards Mars.

And the fireworks would begin. All that he would have to worry about then would be getting himself aboard the Ranger ship without being detected.

Which was impossible, of course. With guards at the #3 lock, nothing could get aboard that they wouldn't know about. Even supposing he could manage it, there were no large storage holds in the Ranger to offer concealment, no good place for a stowaway to hide on the ship.

Was there any other way? Tom wracked his brains and —suddenly—he had it! Yes, there *was* another way. There was one place no one would think of looking for him if he could manage to keep out of range of the view screen lenses— the outer hull of the ship. If he could clamp himself to the hull, somehow, and manage to cling there during blast-off, he could follow Greg and Johnny right home.

He checked the fuse on the airlock once again to make certain it would work. Then he waited, hidden behind the little scout ship's hull, until the orbit ship swung around into shadow. He checked his suit dials: oxygen for twenty-two hours, heater pack fully charged, soda ash only half saturated—it would do. Above him he could see the rear jets of

the Ranger. He swung out onto the orbit ship's hull, and
began to crawl up toward the enemy ship.

It was slow going. Every pressure suit had magnetic boots
and hand-pads to enable crewmen to go outside and make
repairs on the hull of a ship in transit. Tom clung, and moved,
and clung again, trying to reach the protecting hull of the
Ranger before the orbit ship swung him around to the sun
side again.

He couldn't move fast enough. He saw the line of sunlight
coming around the ship as it swung full into the sun. He
froze, crouching motionless. If somebody on the Ranger spotted him now, all would be over. He was exposed like a
lizard on a rock. He waited, hardly daring to breathe, as the
ship spun ponderously around, carrying him into shadow
again.

Nothing happened. He started to crawl upward again,
reached up to grab the mooring cable, and swung himself
across to the hull of the Ranger. The airlock hung open; he
scuttled behind it, clinging to the hull in its shadow just as
Greg and Johnny were herded across by the Jupiter Equilateral guards.

Then he waited. There was no sound, no sign of life. After
a while the Ranger's inner lock opened, and a group of men
hurried across to the orbit ship. Probably a searching party,
Tom thought. Soon the men came back, then returned to the
orbit ship. After another minute, he felt the vibration of the
Scavenger's motors, and he knew that his snare had been
triggered.

He saw the little ship break free and streak out in its curving trajectory. He saw the homing shells burst from the
Ranger's tubes. The Scavenger vanished from his range of
vision, but moments later he saw the sudden flare of light

reflected against the hull of the orbit ship, and he knew his plan had worked.

He waited then until the three searchers returned to the Ranger. Everything in the plan had worked to this point, but the ordeal lay ahead.

And at the end of it, he might really be a dead man.


Hours later, the last group of looters left the orbit ship, and the airlock to the Ranger clanged shut. Tom heard the sucking sound of the airtight seals, then silence. The orbit ship was empty, its insides gutted, its engines no longer operable. The Ranger hung like a long splinter of silver alongside her hull, poised and ready to move on.

Tom knew that the time had come. Very soon the blast-off and the acceleration would begin. He had a few moments to find a position of safety, no more.

Quickly, he began to scramble toward the rear of the Ranger's hull, hugging the metal sides, moving sideways like a crab. Ahead, he knew, the view-screen lenses would be active; if one of them picked him up, it would be quite a jolt to the men inside the ship, and it would be the end of his free ride.

But the major peril was the blast-off. Once the engines cut off, the ship would be in free-fall. Then he could cling easily to the hull, walk all over it if he chose, with the aid of his boots and hand-pads. But unless he found a way to anchor himself firmly to the hull during blast-off, he could be flung off like a pebble. He would never be seen if that happened. Either the jet would catch him, or he would be left hanging in space, with nothing to do but wait for his oxygen supply to be exhausted, and the end would come swiftly then.

He heard a whirring sound and saw the magnetic mooring cables jerk. The ship was preparing for blast-off. Automatic motors were drawing the cables and grappling plates into the hull. Moving quickly, Tom reached the rear cable. Here was his anchor, something to hold him tight to the hull! With one hand he loosened the web belt of his suit and looped it over a corner of the grappling plate as it pulled in to the hull.

The plate pulled tight against the belt. Each plate fit into a shallow excavation in the hull, fitting so snugly that the plates were all but invisible when they were in place. Tom felt himself pulled in tight as the plate gripped the belt against the metal, and the whirring of the motor stopped.

For an instant it looked like the answer. The belt was firmly wedged. He couldn't possibly pull loose without ripping its nylon webbing. But a moment later the motor started to whir again. The plate pushed out from the hull a few inches, then started back, again pulling in the belt.

A good idea that just wouldn't work. The automatic machinery on a space ship was built to perfection; nothing could be permitted to half-work. Tom realized what was happening. Unless the plate fit perfectly in its place, the cable motor could not shut off, and presently an alarm signal would start flashing on the control panel.

He pulled the belt loose, reluctantly. He would have to count on his boots and his hand-pads alone.

He searched the rear hull, looking for some break in the polished metal that might serve as a toe hold. To the rear the fins flared out, supported by heavy struts. He made his way back, crouching close to the hull, and straddled one of the struts. He jammed his magnetic boots down against the hull, and wrapped his arms around the strut with all his strength.

Clinging there, he waited.

It wasn't a good position. The metal of the strut was polished and slick, but it was better than trying to cling to the open hull. He tensed now, not daring to relax for fear that the blast-off acceleration would slam him when he was unprepared.

Deep in the ship, the engines began to rumble. He felt it rather than heard it, a low-pitched vibration that grew stronger and stronger. The Ranger would not need a great thrust to move away from the orbit ship, but if they were in a hurry, they might start out at nearly Mars-escape.

The jets flared, and something slammed him down against the fin strut. The Ranger moved out, its engines roaring, accelerating hard. Tom felt as though he had been hit by a ton of rock. The strut seemed to press in against his chest; he could not breath. His hands were sliding, and he felt the pull on his boots. He tightened his grip desperately. This was it. He had to hang on, *had* to hang on. . . .

He saw his boot on the hull surface, sliding slowly, creeping back and stretching his leg. Suddenly it broke loose; he lurched to one side, and the other boot began sliding. The ache in his arms was terrible, as though some malignant giant were tearing at him, trying to wrench him loose as he fought for his hold.

There was one black instant when he felt he could not hold on another second. He could see the blue flame of the jet streaming behind him and the cold blackness of space beyond that. It had been a fool's idea, he thought in despair, a million-to-one shot that he had taken, and lost. . . .

And then the pressure stopped. His boots clanged down

on the hull, and he almost lost his hand-grip. He stretched an arm, shook himself, took a great painful breath, and clung to the strut, almost sobbing, hardly daring to move.

The ordeal was over. Somewhere, far ahead, an orbit ship was waiting for the Ranger to return. He would have to be ready for the braking thrust and the side-maneuvering thrusts, but he would manage to hold on. Crouching against the fin, he would be invisible to viewers on the orbit ship, and who would be looking for a man clinging to the outside of a scout ship?

Tom sighed, and waited. Jupiter Equilateral would have its prisoners, all right. He wished now that he had not discarded the stunner, but those extra pounds might have made the difference between life and death during the blast-off. He was not completely unarmed though. He still had Dad's revolver at his side.

He smiled to himself. The pirates would have their prisoners, indeed, but they would also have one factor to deal with that they had not counted on.

For Greg it was a bitter, lonely trip. Johnny was there, of course, and occasionally they exchanged a word or two, but the guards were always nearby, watching, listening. And after all, what was there to say?

They knew the ship was moving deeper into the belt. Six hours passed, eight, ten. Suddenly there was a flurry of activity in the control cabin. A sighting was recorded, the crew strapped down, and the braking jets were fired.

They saw the huge Jupiter Equilateral orbit ship loom up in the view screen like a minor planet. Skillfully, Doc maneu-

vered the ship into the launching rack. The guards unstrapped the prisoners and handed them pressure suits.

Moments later they were moving through the airlock into
the main corridor of the big orbit ship. "Move along, now,"
Doc was saying. "And no tricks. Be a pity to have to mark
you up after all this trouble."

In a section in the crew's quarters they stripped off their
suits. This orbit ship was much larger than Roger Hunter's;
the gravity was almost Mars-normal, and it was comforting
just to stretch and relax cramped muscles.

As long as they didn't think of what was ahead.

Finally Johnny grinned and slapped Greg's shoulder.
"Cheer up," he said. "We'll be honored guests for a while,
you can bet on that."

"For a while," Greg repeated bitterly.

"Well, we may be able to stretch that while out a bit,"
Johnny said. He looked to make sure the guard wasn't listening. "We don't know what they think we do, but they don't
know that. We may be able to string them along for a while.
Meanwhile, we might just get a break."

"Maybe," Greg said. "I don't know how, but maybe."

They were just slipping out of their suits when the hatchway opened. "Well, whom do we have here?" a familiar voice
said. "Returning a call, you might say. And maybe this time
you'll be ready for a bit of bargaining."

They turned to see the heavy face and angry eyes of
Merrill Tawney.

## Chapter Eight

## THE SCAVENGERS OF SPACE

THE casual observer might have been fooled. Tawney's guard was down only for an instant; then the expression of cold fury and determination dropped away as though the shutter of a camera had clicked, and he was all smiles and affability. They were honored guests here, one would have thought, and this pudgy agent of the Jupiter Equilateral combine was their genial host, anxious for their welfare, eager to do anything he could for their comfort.

But Greg had seen the mask dropped into place, and caught a momentary glimpse of the viciousness underneath. He had known people like this before, the ones who hid behind smiles, and he had always hated them. Now every instinct screamed at him to throw himself at the fat little company man, but he fought down the impulse, clenching his fists at his sides.

Tawney was talking as he led them out into the corridor. "The trip was comfortable, I hope? Of course, those scout ships are always cramped, but you'll find things here much more commodious." He stopped beside a small oval shuttle car that hung from a single track overhead. "You may be surprised at the size of this ship, it's a fully equipped city in space, really. These cars save hours of transit time."

He motioned them into the front seats, then climbed into the rear with the guard. The car started up, moving swiftly through a maze of corridors. They crossed from the outer level through several of the inner levels before the car slid to a halt, and Tawney ushered them through a hatchway.

In spite of himself, Greg's mouth fell open in amazement. He had never seen such luxury in a space ship; there was hardly an apartment in all of Sun Lake City that matched the richness of the room they were standing in. It was a beautiful lounge; thick carpeting covered the metal deck plates. There were soft chairs, pleasant, concealed lighting, paintings on the walls. A table was set at one side, and a white-coated steward hovered near by. Real Earth-side beefsteaks were sizzling on the grill. Greg suddenly remembered that they hadn't eaten in over twelve hours and found the aroma of food tantalizing.

Tawney smiled, rubbing his hands together. "I suppose you've been thinking that you'd be kept in a cell, and starved and tortured, and things like that, eh? But we don't believe in doing things that way. Let's just say you're my guests. Some food now, and then we can talk."

He left them, and the guard retired to the far end of the lounge. Johnny looked at the steaks and shrugged. "We might as well eat," he said. "No sense in starvin' ourselves. We're likely to be here for a long time, and if we get a chance to make a break, we'll need our strength."

They dug in. The steaks were perfect, the first real steaks that Greg had ever eaten. "What do you think Tawney has in mind?" he asked between bites. "Why all the red carpet treatment?"

"Just enjoy it while it lasts," Johnny advised, "but don't get carried away. Tawney is Tawney, red carpet or no red carpet. Tawney wants somethin' and he wants it bad. Once he gets it—" Johnny drew his finger across his throat, and took another bite of steak.

They were finishing their second cup of coffee when Tawney returned. "Feeling better, gentlemen?"

"You do things in a big way," Johnny said. "This is real coffee, made from *coffee beans*. Must have cost a fortune to ship it out here."

Tawney spread his hands. "We keep it for special occasions. Like when we have special visitors."

"Even when the visits aren't voluntary," Greg added sourly.

"We have to be realistic," Tawney said. "Would you have come if we invited you? Of course not. You gentlemen chose to come out to the belt in spite of my warnings. You thus made things very awkward for us, upset certain of our plans." He looked at Greg. "We don't ordinarily allow people to upset our plans, but now we find that we're forced to include you in our plans, whether you happen to like the idea or not."

"You're doing a lot of talking," Greg said. "Why don't you come to the point?"

"I think you know the point," Tawney said.

"I'm pretty stupid," Greg said. "I like to have things spelled out."

"Then I'll spell it out for you." Tawney was no longer smiling. "We happen to know that your father struck a rich lode on one of his claims."

"That's interesting," Greg said. "Did Dad tell you that?"

"He didn't have to. A man can't keep a secret like that, not for very long. Ask your friend here, if you don't believe me. And we make it our business to know what's going on out here. We have to, in order to survive."

"Well, suppose you heard right. The law says that what a man finds on his own claim is his."

"Certainly," Tawney said. "Nobody would think of claim jumping, these days. But when a man happens to die before he can bring in his bonanza, then it's a question of who gets there first, wouldn't you think?"

"Not when the man is murdered," Greg said hotly, "not by a long shot."

"But you can't prove that your father was murdered."

"If I could, I wouldn't be here."

"Then I think we'll stick to the law," Tawney said, "and call it an accident."

"And what about my brother? Was that an accident?"

"Ah, yes, your brother." Tawney's eyes hardened. "Quite a different matter, that. Sometimes Doc tends to be over-zealous in carrying out his assigned duties. I can assure you that he has been . . . disciplined."

"That's not going to help Tom very much."

"Unfortunately not," Tawney said. "Your brother made a very foolish move, under the circumstances. But from a practical point of view, perhaps it's not entirely a tragedy."

"What do you mean by that?"

"From what I've heard," Tawney said, "you didn't have much use for your twin brother. So now you won't have to share your father's legacy—"

It was too much. With a roar Greg swung at the little fat

man. The blow caught Tawney full in the jaw, jerked his head back. Greg threw his shoulder into a hard left, slamming Tawney back against the wall. The guard charged across the room, dragging them apart as Tawney blubbered and tried to cover his face. Greg dug his elbow into the guard's stomach, twisted away and started for Tawney again. Then Johnny caught his arm and spun him around. "Stop it," he snapped. "Use your head, boy!"

Greg stopped, glaring at Tawney and gasping for breath. The company man picked himself up, rubbing his hand across his mouth. For a moment he trembled with rage. Then he gripped the table with one hand, forcibly regaining his control. He even managed a sickly smile. "Just like your father," he said, "too hot-headed for your own good. But we'll let it pass. I brought you here to make you an offer, a very generous offer, and I'll still make it. I'm a businessman. When I want something I bargain for it. If I have to share a profit to get it, I share the profit. All right. You know where your father's strike is. We want it. We can't find it, so you've got us over a barrel. We're ready to bargain."

Greg started forward. "I wouldn't bargain with you for—"

"Shut up, Greg," Johnny said.

Greg stared at him. The big miner's voice had cracked like a whip. He drew Merrill Tawney aside and spoke rapidly into his ear. Tawney listened, shot a venomous glance across at Greg, and finally nodded. "All right," he said, "but I can't wait forever."

"You won't have to."

Tawney turned to the guard. "You have your orders," he said. "They're to have these quarters and the freedom of the ship, except for the outer level. They're not to be harmed, and they're not to be out of your sight except when they're locked in here. Is that clear?"

The guard nodded. Tawney looked at Johnny, and started for the door, still rubbing his jaw. "We'll talk again later," he said, and left.

When the guard also left and the lock buzzed in the door, Johnny looked at Greg and shook his head sadly. "You just about fixed things, boy, you really did."

"Well, what was I supposed to do, just stand there and listen to him?" Greg turned away angrily. "What did you say to him to quiet him down so fast?"

"I said I'd talk you into a deal with him, but I needed time," Johnny said.

"You'll need time, all right," Greg said. "If you think I'd deal with him—"

"Of course I don't," Johnny said. "I just want to stay alive a while, that's all. Look, there isn't goin' to be any bargainin' with Tawney, he just doesn't work that way. It's heads he wins, tails we lose. Once he has what he wants we won't last six minutes. All right. Then there's just one thing that can keep us alive—stallin' him. He thinks you know what he wants to know, and as long as he thinks so, he won't touch us. We've got to squeeze every minute out of it that we can. We've got to make him think you'll give in if he plays his cards right."

Greg was silent for a minute. "I hadn't thought of it that way."

"Well, you'd better start thinkin', then. As soon as Tawney tumbles to what we're doing, things are goin' to get pretty ugly around here, and nobody's goin' to help us. We've got to use the time we have to find some way to break for it." Johnny stood up, staring around the luxurious lounge. "And if you want my opinion, it's going to take some pretty fancy footwork to get out of here with our skins."

Miles across the blackness of space there was a sudden flare of blue-white light, growing from a brilliant pinpoint into an expanding fireball that lighted up the prisoners' faces as they watched it on the view screen.

Slowly then, the light faded. A section of the screen went telescopic, and suddenly they could see the aftermath of the explosion in sharp focus before their eyes.

They had been watching the death of an asteroid. For over an hour the final preparations had been taking place; then, minutes before the explosion, they had seen the work crews move away from the rock on scooters, to take refuge in the near-by scout ship.

"It's a pretty good-sized rock," the guard told them as they waited for the blast. "Seven and four-tenths miles mean diameter, bigger than most of them. We've had crews working there for three shifts, placing the charges just right for maximum fragmentation. Of course, we'll still have fragments too large for processing, but we can crush them up with single charges later. Now watch this."

The tiny scout ship was moving back into view again as the fragments of the asteroid spun out in an expanding cloud. But now the ship was unfurling behind it a huge glittering net of magnetic wire that opened out like a gigantic spider web. The scout ship swung into a wide arc around the cloud of asteroid fragments, then moved slowly forward, drawing in the net.

It looked ridiculously like the old pictures of Earth-side fishermen at work. Anything other than a controlled Murexide explosion would have sent the asteroid fragments spinning away in all directions at a speed so great that they could never have been corralled and salvaged. Greg could remember his father's stories of the early days of asteroid mining, when the old-type uranium charges were used. In those days the magnetic net was spread around the rock before it was blown up; too often the charges would be too powerful, sending huge radioactive fragments ripping through the nets, and tearing scout ships to shreds in space.

Many men had died mining in the belt in those days. Now the controlled charges exerted just the force necessary to split the rocks into fragments, and no more, but the job of netting the fragments still depended on the skill of the scout ship's navigator-pilot team.

They were watching such a team in action now, and Greg shook his head in grudging admiration as the pilot of the little scout darted back and forth, weaving the net around the slowly escaping fragments, drawing them in, moving again, until at last all but the tiniest bits of broken rock were engulfed in the net.

Then the scout ship moved into a slow arc back toward the orbit ship, drawing its net behind it.

This was asteroid mining. The same techniques were used by the huge mining companies and the tiny independents alike, but few of the independents had the top-grade equipment, the man power or the sheer engineering skill to do the sort of slick professional job that Johnny and Greg were witnessing now.

True to his word, Tawney had given them the freedom of the ship. Greg and Johnny discovered that their guard was also an excellent guide. All day he had been leading them through the ship, chatting and answering their questions, until they almost forgot that they were prisoners here. And the guard's obvious pride in the scope and skill of his company's mining operations was strangely infectious.

Certainly the orbit ship was an excellent headquarters; it lacked nothing as a base for mining operations. Orbiting in an asteroid cluster chosen for the high density of asteroids in the vicinity, the ship buzzed with activity like a nest of hornets. Two dozen scout ships nestled at the side of the huge ship, shooting out to their various sites of operation, buzzing back with glittering nets in tow, pulling in asteroid fragments. Down in the storage holds crews of workmen were sorting the fragments, analyzing them in the compact assay lab, separating them into high-grade and low-grade ores for the smelters on Earth and Mars.

When a particularly high-grade ore turned up in a batch, the whole ship hummed with excitement. "We take our chances, just like the independents," the guard told them. "Each man gets his percentage of the earnings on every trip. Give us one big strike, and everybody on this ship will be rich."

"Do you pick and choose your rocks?" Johnny asked.

"Oh, yes. We have prospectors working all over the belt, claiming the best-looking rocks for the company. When they hit something rich, an orbit ship moves in to work it." The guard laughed. "You should hear the astronomers hoot at us, the ones that go for the incomplete-formation theory of the asteroids. They say we'll never hit a big strike because no such thing can exist. But we don't pay any attention to them."

Greg was familiar with the story. Every schoolboy on Mars knew about the two opposing theories of formation which attempted to solve once and for all the age-old mystery of how the Asteroid Belt had been formed. Many astronomers believed that the asteroids were fragments of a planet that had never formed completely, that while the other planets in the solar system were forming, these chunks of debris had been held apart and kept from coalescing into a planet by the overwhelming gravitational pull of the giant planet lying just beyond the belt. . . . Jupiter itself.

But an older theory held that the asteroids had once been a fully formed planet between Mars and Jupiter, a planet that had been blown apart geological ages before in a series of cataclysmic explosions. Gradually the fragments of those explosions had taken up their individual orbits as tiny planetoids in a wide belt around the sun where the parent planet had once been. What might have caused those explosions nobody could guess, nor could anyone guess what sort of planet it might have been.

Which theory was right, nobody knew. When the solar system was first explored, the asteroids had been eagerly studied in hopes that the true answer might be found. But as yet neither side could claim the answer. The mystery remained unsolved.

Greg had thought about it many times. If there *had* been a planet here, hundreds of thousands of years ago, what had it been like? Had it been warm, as Earth was now, with an atmosphere, perhaps even with life on it? Or was it a barren rock, free of atmosphere, as dead and lifeless as Earth's moon? What could have caused it to explode? There were no answers, and the fragments, the asteroids themselves, had never yielded a clue.

Now Greg watched as the scout ship moved in to the orbit ship's side with its net. Whatever the origin of the asteroids, these fragments of rock contained rich metal waiting to be taken by the men who could find it. Watching the Jupiter

Equilateral ship in operation, Greg felt his heart sink. Here was a huge, powerful organization, with all the equipment and men and know-how they could ever need. How could one man, or two or even a team of three hope to compete with them? For the independent miner, the only hope was the big strike, the single lode that could make him rich. He might work all his life without finding it, and then stumble upon it by sheer chance.

But if he couldn't keep it when he found it, what then? What if the great mining company became so strong that they could be their own law in the belt? What if they grew strong enough and powerful enough to challenge the United Nations on Mars itself, and gain control of the entire mining industry? What chance would the independent miner have then?

It was a frightening picture. Suddenly something began to make sense to Greg; he realized something about his father that he had never known before. Roger Hunter had been a miner, yes. But he had been something else too, something far more important than just a miner. Roger Hunter had been a fighter, fighting to the end for something he believed in.

The scout ship shot out its grappling cables as Greg and Johnny watched in the view screen. Merrill Tawney was in the observation room, watching too. The first scout ship moored and secured; from another direction another ship came in with a loaded net. Tawney rubbed his hands together.

"Quite an operation," he said.

Greg looked at him. "So I see."

"And very efficient, too. Our men have everything they

need to work with. We can mine at far less cost than anyone else."

"But you still can't stand the idea of independent miners working the belt," Greg said.

Tawney's eyebrows went up. "Why not? There's lots of room out here. Our operation with Jupiter Equilateral is no different from an independent miner's operation. We aren't different kinds of people." He smiled. "When you get right down to it, we're both exactly the same thing—scavengers in space, vultures picking over the dead remains to see what we can find. We come out to the asteroids, and we bring back what we want and leave the rest behind. And it doesn't matter whether we've got one ship working or four hundred, we're still scavengers."

"With just one difference," Greg said, turning away from the view screen.

"Difference?"

Greg nodded. "Even vultures don't kill their prey," he said.

Later, when they were again alone in their quarters, Greg and Johnny stared at each other gloomily. For all its luxurious appointments, the place was a prison. The only sound was the intermittent whir of the ventilator fan in the wall. The single hatchway was locked, and they knew that the guard was stationed in the corridor outside.

Johnny had even found a microphone pickup hidden in one of the chair cushions; he had carefully disconnected it, and they had poked and probed to find any others that might be there. But the rest of the furniture was innocent enough; except for the fine metal grill over the ventilator shaft the walls were featureless.

"Didn't you see *anything* that might help us?" Greg asked.

"Not much. For an orbit ship, this place is a fortress. I got a good look at that scout ship coming in. It was armed to the teeth. Prob'bly they all are. And they're keepin' a guard now at every airlock."

"So we're sewed up tight," Greg said.

"Looks that way. They've got us, boy, and I think Tawney's patience is wearing thin, too. We're either going to have to produce or else."

"But what can we do?"

"Start bluffin'."

"It seems to me we're just about bluffed out."

"I mean talk business," Johnny said. "Tell Tawney what he wants to know."

"When we don't know any more than he does? How?"

Johnny Coombs scratched his jaw. "I've been thinking about that," he said slowly, "and I wonder if we don't know a whole lot more than we think we do."

"Like what?" Greg said.

"We've all been looking for the same thing—a big strike, a bonanza lode. Tawney's men have raked over every one of your dad's claims, and they haven't turned up a thing." Johnny looked at Greg. "Makes you wonder a little, doesn't it? Your dad was smart, but he was no magician. And how does a man go about hidin' somethin' like a vein of ore?"

"I don't know," Greg said. "It doesn't seem possible."

"It isn't possible," Johnny said flatly. "There's only one possible explanation, and we've been missin' it all along. Whatever he found, *it wasn't an ore strike*. It was somethin' else, something far different from anything we've been thinkin' of."

Greg stared at him. "But if it wasn't an ore strike, what was it?"

"I don't know," Johnny said. "But I'm sure of one thing. It was something so important that he was ready to die before he'd reveal it. And that means it's so important that Tawney won't dare kill us until he finds out what it is."

*Chapter Nine*

---

## THE INVISIBLE MAN

CROUCHING back into the shadow, Tom waited as the heavy footsteps moved up the corridor, then back down, then up and down again. He peered around the corner for a moment, looking quickly up and down the curving corridor. The guard was twenty yards away, moving toward him in a slow measured pace. Tom jerked his head back, then peered out again as the footsteps receded.

The guard was a big man, with a heavy duty stunner resting in the crook of his elbow. He paused, scratched himself, and resumed his pacing. Tom waited, hoping that something might distract the big man, but he moved stolidly back and forth, far too alert for Tom to risk breaking out into the main corridor.

Tom moved back into the darkened corridor where he was standing, trying to decide what to do. It was a side corridor, and a blind alley; it ended in a large hatchway marked HYDROPONICS, and there were no branching corridors. If he were discovered here, there would be no place to hide.

But he knew that he could never hope to accomplish his purpose here.

A hatch clanged open, and there were more footsteps down the main corridor as a change of guards hurried by. There was a rumble of voices, and Tom listened to catch the words.

". . . don't care what you think, the boss says tighten it up."

"But they got them locked in."

"So tell it to the boss. We're supposed to check every compartment in the section every hour. Now get moving."

The footsteps moved up and down the corridor, and Tom heard hatches clanging open. If they sent a light down this spur . . . he turned to the hatch, spun the big wheel on the door, and slipped inside just as the footsteps came closer.

The stench inside was almost overpowering. The big, darkened room was extremely warm, the air damp with vapor. The plastic-coated walls streamed with moisture. Against the walls Tom could see the great hydroponic vats that held the yeast and algae cultures that fed the crew. Water was splashing in one of the vats, and there was a gurgling sound as the nutrient broth was exchanged automatically.

He moved swiftly across the compartment, into a darkened area behind the rows of vats, and crouched down. He heard footsteps, and the ring of metal as the hatchway came open. One of the guards walked in, peered into the gloom, wrinkled his nose, and walked out again, closing the hatchway behind him.

It would do for a while if he didn't suffocate, but if this ship was organized like smaller ones, it would be a blind alley. Modern hydroponic tanks did not require much servicing, once the cultures were growing; the broth was drained automatically and sluiced through a series of pipes to the rendering plant where the yeasts could be flavored and pressed into surrogate steaks and other foods for space ship cuisine. There would be no other entrances, no way to leave except the way he had come in.

With the guards on duty, that was out of the question. He waited, listening, as the check-down continued in near-by compartments. Then silence fell again. The heavy yeast aroma had grown more and more oppressive; now suddenly a fan went on with a whir, and a cool draft of freshened, re-processed air poured down from the ventilator shaft above his head.

Getting into the orbit ship had been easier than Tom had hoped. In the excitement, as the new prisoners were brought aboard, security measures had been lax. No one had expected a third visitor; in consequence, no one looked for one. Huge as it was, the Jupiter Equilateral ship had never been planned as a prison, and it had taken time to stake out the guards in a security system that was at all effective. In addition, every man who served as a guard had been taken from duty somewhere else on the ship.

So there had been no guard at the airlock in the first few moments after the prisoners were taken off the Ranger ship. Tom had waited until the ship was moored, clinging to the fin strut. He watched Greg and Johnny being taken through the lock, and soon the last of the crew had crossed over after securing the ship. Presently the orbit ship's airlock had gone dark, and only then had he ventured from his place of con-cealment, creeping along the dark hull of the Ranger ship and leaping across to the airlock.

A momentary risk, then, as he opened the lock. In the con-trol room, he knew, a signal light would blink on a panel as the lock was opened. Tom moved as quickly as he could, hoping that in the excitement of the new visitors, the signal would go unnoticed, or if spotted, that the spotter would assume it was only a crewman making a final trip across to the Ranger ship.

But once inside, he began to realize the magnitude of his problem. This was not a tiny independent orbit ship with a few corridors and compartments. This was a huge ship, a vast complex of corridors and compartments and holds. There was probably a crew of a thousand men on this ship, and there was no sign of where Greg and Johnny might have been taken.

He moved forward, trying to keep to side corridors and darkened areas. In the airlock he had wrapped up his pressure suit and stored it on a rack; no one would notice it there, and it might be handy later. He had strapped his father's gun case to his side—a comfort, but a small one.

Now, crouching behind the yeast vat, he lifted out the gun, hefted it idly in his hand. It was a weapon, at least. He was not well acquainted with guns, and in the shadowy light it seemed to him that this one looked odd for a revolver; it even felt wrong, out of balance in his hand. He slipped it back in the case. After all, it had been fitted to Dad's hand, not his. And Johnny or Greg would know how to use it better than he did—if he could find them.

But to do that he would have to search the ship. He would have to move about, he couldn't just wait in a storage hold. And with all the guards that were posted, he would certainly stumble into one of them sooner or later if he tried leaving this spot. He shook his head, and started for the hatch. He would have to chance it. There was no way to tell how much time he had, but it was a sure bet that he didn't have very long.

In the spur corridor again, he waited until the guard's footsteps were muffled and distant. Then he darted out into the main corridor, moving swiftly and silently away from the guard. At the first hatchway he ducked inside and waited in the darkness, panting.

The guard stopped walking. Then his footsteps resumed, but more quickly, coming down the corridor. He stopped, almost outside the hatchway door. "Funny," Tom heard him mutter. "I'd have sworn—"

Tom held his breath, waiting. This was a storage hold, but he didn't dare move, even to take cover. The guard stood motionless for a moment, grunted, and resumed his slow pacing. When he had moved away Tom caught his breath in huge gasps, his heart beating in his throat. It was no use, he thought in despair. Once or twice he might get away with it, but sooner or later a guard would be alert enough to investigate an obscure noise, a flicker of movement in the corner of his eye.

There had to be another way. His eye probed the storage hold, hopelessly, and stopped on a metal grill in the wall.

For a moment, he didn't recognize what it was. He heard a *whoosh-whoosh-whoosh* as a fan went on, and he felt cool air against his cheek. He held out his hand to the grill and found the air coming from there.

It was a ventilation shaft. Every space craft had to have reconditioning units for the air inside the ship. The men inside needed a constant supply of fresh oxygen; but even more, without pumps to move the air in each compartment, they would soon suffocate from the accumulation of carbon dioxide in the air they breathed out, or bake from the heat their bodies radiated. On the other hand, the yeasts and algae required carbon dioxide and yielded copious amounts of oxygen as they grew.

In Roger Hunter's little orbit ship the ventilation shafts were small, a loose network of foot-square ducts leading from the central pumps and air-reconditioning units to every compartment in the ship. But in a ship of this size—

The grill was over a yard wide, four feet tall. It started about shoulder height and ran up to the overhead. The ducts would network the ship, opening into every compartment, and no one would ever open them unless something went wrong.

He grinned happily as he got busy, working the grill out of the slots that held it to the wall and trying to keep his hands from shaking in his excitement.

He knew he had found his answer.

The grill came loose and Tom lifted it down in one piece. He stopped short as footsteps approached in the corridor, paused, and went on. Then he peered into the black gaping hole behind the grill. It was big enough for a man to crawl in. He shinnied up into the hole, and pulled the grill back into its slot behind him.

Somewhere far away he heard a throbbing of giant pumps. There was a rush of cool fresh air past his cheek, cold when it contacted the sweat pouring down his forehead. He could not quite stand up, but there was plenty of room for him to crouch and move.

Ahead of him was a black tunnel, broken only by a patch of light coming through the grill that opened into the next compartment. He stared into the blackness, his heart racing.

Somewhere in the ship Johnny and Greg were prisoners, but now, Tom knew, there was a way to escape.

It was a completely different world, a world within a world, a world of darkness and silence, of a thousand curving and intersecting tunnels, some large, some small. For hours it seemed to Tom that he had been wandering through a tomb, moving through the corridors of a dead ship, the lone surviving crewman. There was some contact with the other world, of course, the world of the space ship outside. Each compartment had its metal grill, and he passed many of them. But these were like doors that only he knew existed. He met no one in *these* corridors, there was no danger of sudden discovery and arrest in these dark alleys.

His boots had made too much noise when he started out, so he had slipped them off, hanging them from his belt and moving on in his stocking feet. As he went from duct to duct, he had an almost ridiculous feeling of freedom and power. In every sense, he was an invisible man. Not one soul on this great ship knew he was here, or even suspected it. He had the run of the ship, complete freedom to go wherever he chose. He could move from compartment to compartment as silently and invisibly as if he had no substance at all.

He knew his first job was to learn the pattern of the ducts, and orientation was a problem. He had heard stories of men getting lost in the deep underground mining tunnels on Mars, wandering in circles for days until their food gave out and they starved. And there was that hazard here, for every duct looked like every other one.

Yet there was a difference, because the ducts curved just as the main ship's corridors did. He could always identify the center of the ship by the force of false gravity pulling the other way. Furthermore, as the ducts drew closer to the pumps and reconditioning units, they opened into larger vents, and the noise of the pumps thundered in his ears. After an hour of exploration, Tom was certain that from any place in the ship he could at least find his way to the outer layer, and from there to one of the scout ship's airlocks.

Finding Greg and Johnny was a different matter.

He could not see enough through the compartment grills to identify just what the compartments were; he was forced to rely on what he could hear. The engine rooms were easily identified. In one area he heard the banging of pots and pans, the steaming of kettles—obviously the galley. From the storage holds came a vast silence, broken by a rumbling crash as ore poured down the metal chutes for storage.

He found the crew's living quarters and paused at one compartment as voices came through the grill. A man with a squeaky voice was complaining bitterly about his turn on guard; a deeper voice was more philosophical. "Be too bad if they broke out somehow, after all this work," he was saying.

"You think they're going to talk?" the squeaky voice asked.

"Sure they'll talk. What else can they do?"

"Maybe they'll just clam up and thumb their noses at the boss," Squeaky said.

The other laughed. "That I'd like to see, somebody thumbing his nose at the boss! Don't worry, they'll talk, and when they do there'll be enough to take care of everybody."

"Well, maybe," Squeaky said, not too convinced. "I still wish they hadn't blasted that other one."

"You scared of ghosts or something?"

"No, but if something went wrong, the whole crew might be held."

"Don't worry. The U.N. can't touch us. The boss has got 'em running. Why, ten years ago they'd have been out here questioning every outfit in the belt after they found the old man's body. And what do they do now? Nothing, that's what."

Tom moved on, grinning to himself. The man was right, of course. Nothing had been done about Roger Hunter's death, nothing much, not yet.

But the fun hadn't even started.

He kept moving, stopping to listen at each grill. At one point, as he moved in toward the center of the ship, his wrist Geiger began to sputter. He stopped and turned back, making a wide circle around the area. He knew that a separate system of ventilators handled the radioactive waste gases when the engines were in operation, but there was no need to venture into those regions.

Later, he found the control area. He could hear the clatter of typing instruments, the *click-click-click* of the computers working out the orbits and trajectories for the scout ships as they moved out from the orbit ship or came back in. In another compartment he heard a dispatcher chattering his own special code-language into a microphone in a low-pitched voice. He passed another grill, and then stopped short as a familiar voice drifted through.

Merrill Tawney's voice.

Tom hugged the grill, straining to catch the words. The company man sounded angry; the man he was talking to sounded even angrier. "I can't help what you want or don't want, Merrill, I can only report what we've found, and that's nothing at all. Every one of those claims has been searched twice over. Doc and his boys went over them, and we didn't find anything they might have missed. I think you're barking up the wrong tree."

"There's *got* to be something," Tawney said, his voice tight with anger. "Hunter couldn't have taken anything away from there, he didn't have a chance to. You read the reports."

"I know," the other said wearily, "I know what the reports said."

"Then what he found is still there. There's no other possibility," Tawney said.

"We went over that rock with a microscope. We blew it to shreds. Assay has gone through the fragments literally piece by piece. They found low-grade iron, a trace of nickel, a little tin. And just lots and lots of granite. If we never found anything richer than that, we'd have been out of business ten years ago."

There was a long silence. Tom pressed closer to the grill. He heard Tawney slam his fist into his palm. "You know what Roger Hunter's doing, don't you?" he cried. "He's making fools of us, that's what! The man's dead, and he's making us look like idiots. If we hadn't been so sure we had the lode spotted—" He broke off. "Well, that's done; we can't undo it. But this brat of his—"

"Any luck there?"

"Not a word. He's playing hard to get."

"Maybe he doesn't know anything. Doc made a bad mistake when he blasted the other one. Suppose *he* was the only one who knew."

"All right, it was a mistake," Tawney snapped. "What was Doc supposed to do? Let the boy get back to Mars? We've got a good front there, but it's not that good. If the United Nations gets a toe hold out here, the whole belt will go into their pocket; you realize that. They're waiting for us to make one slip." He paused, and Tom heard him pacing the compartment. "But I think we've got our boy. This one knows. We've been spoiling him so far, that's all. Well, now we start digging. When I get through with him, he'll be begging us to let him tell. You just watch me, as soon as the okay comes through."

Tom drew back from the grill, moving on in the darkness. So far he had not rushed his exploration. If there was a chance to use the ducts for escape, he wanted to know them well. But now he knew the hour was getting late. So far Greg and Johnny had been stalling Tawney, but Tawney was getting impatient.

He moved quickly, stopping at each compartment only long enough to identify it. Crew's quarters, the executive suite, officers' quarters—nowhere was there a sign of the prisoners. He found himself retracing his steps, listening more closely. Unless he could locate them, he was helpless.

But he thought again of what Tawney had said. Tawney was right about one thing. There was no way that Dad could have hidden a big strike so nobody could find it. It had to be there.

And yet it wasn't. He and Greg hadn't found it. Tawney's men hadn't found it, either. Why not? There must be a reason. But he could not put his finger on it.

Half an hour later he was seriously worried. Half the compartments in the area he was exploring were deserted, the men leaving for the cafeteria. The thought reminded Tom how hungry he was, and thirsty. His small emergency ration kit was empty. He toyed with the thought of sneaking into a food storage compartment, then thrust it out of his mind as too risky. He had to find Greg and Johnny before doing anything else.

He passed a grill, and heard a murmur of voices. Something in the deep bass rumble caught his ear. He stopped, listened.

The voices stopped also.

He waited for them to begin, pressing against the grill. Johnny Coombs was not the only man with a deep bass voice. Tom might have been mistaken. He listened, but there was no sound. He heard the whir of a fan begin. Still no sound, not even footsteps.

And then it happened, so fast he was taken completely off guard. The grill suddenly gave way, pitching him forward into the compartment. Something struck him behind the ear as he fell; there was a grunt, a sharp command, and he was pinned to the floor in the semidarkness of the compartment.

He heard a gasp and opened his eyes. He was staring into his brother's unbelieving, startled face. Greg was pinning his shoulders to the carpeted deck, and behind him Johnny Coombs had a fist raised.

But they had stopped in mid-air, like a tableau of puppets. Greg gaped, his jaw falling open, and Tom heard himself saying, "What are you trying to do, kill a guy? Seems to me one time is enough."

He had found them.

*Chapter Ten*

---

## TOM PULLS THE TRIGGER

IN the first instant of recognition Greg and Johnny were speechless. Later, Tom said it was the first time in his life that he had ever seen Greg totally without words. His brother jumped back as if he had seen a ghost. His mouth worked, but no sounds came out.

"Don't worry, it's me all right," Tom said, "and I'm mighty hungry."

Greg and Johnny stared at the black hole behind the grill, and then Greg was pummeling him, pounding him on the back, so excited he couldn't get a word out. And Johnny was hovering over them, incredulous, but forced to believe his eyes, like a father overwhelmed by the impossible behavior of a pair of unpredictable children. It was a jubilant reunion all around. They ransacked the cabinets and refrigerator in the back of the lounge and pulled out surro-ham and rolls, while Johnny got some coffee going. Tom was so famished he could hardly wait to make sandwiches of the ham. Finally he slowed up and got his mouth empty enough to talk.

"All right, let's have the story," Greg said, still looking as though he couldn't believe his eyes. "The last we saw, you were blown into atoms out there in that *Scavenger*. You've got some nerve turning up now and scaring us half out of our skins."

"You want me to go back in my hole?"

"Just sit still and talk!"

Tom talked, starting from the beginning: his realization that the battle for their father's orbit ship was a lost cause; his reasoning that if all three were captured, there would be little chance for escape; his determination to "play dead", to make the raiders think he had been destroyed—there was nothing he left out. "I only hoped I got the autopilot set right, and the shell-evasion mechanism," he said. "But I didn't have much time to study up on navigation at the time."

"Don't worry, it was realistic enough," Greg said grimly. "The way that little ship went dodging those shells was enough to convince anybody."

"Well, then the trick was to get back here with you." Tom told them about his terrifying ride on the hull of the Ranger, his near-encounter with the guard once he had come aboard the Jupiter Equilateral orbit ship, and his idea of using the ventilation ducts for both concealment and movement. Through it all Greg stared in admiration. "We've got a genius among us, that's all," he said finally. "And I always thought you were the timid one."

"But what else could I do?" Tom asked. "You know what they say about grabbing a tiger by the tail. Once you get hold, you've got to hold on."

"Okay," Greg said, "but the next time I make a crack about your retiring nature, remind me to stick my foot in my mouth."

"I'll do it for him," Johnny Coombs rumbled.

Tom nodded toward the open grill. "The only thing I don't see is how you knew I was back there."

Johnny grinned. "We were busy taking down the grill when you came along. We'd found a microphone in this place, and figured they might have one behind the grill. And then we heard somebody breathing. We thought they'd posted a guard back there, just to snoop on us."

"Well, I'm glad you didn't hit him any harder."

Johnny started to say something and stopped, his head cocked toward the door. Footsteps sounded in the corridor outside; they came closer, stopped by the door. "Quick," Johnny whispered. "Back inside!"

There was no time to look for other concealment. Tom leaped across the room, jumped up into the shaft again, and Greg slammed the grate up into place just as the hatchway door swung open.

Merrill Tawney walked into the room, with two burly guards behind him.

For the first few seconds, Greg was certain that they were lost. He stood with his back to the ventilator grill, frozen in his tracks as the fat little company man came into the room. He tried to keep his face blank, but he knew he wasn't succeeding. He saw the puzzled frown on Tawney's face.

The company man motioned the guards into the room, peered suspiciously at Greg and Johnny. "Am I interrupting something, by any chance?"

"Nothing at all," Johnny blurted. "We were just talking."

"Talking." Tawney repeated the word as if it were in

some strange language he didn't quite understand. He looked at the guard. "Let's just check them."

While one guard patted down their clothes, the other withdrew a stunner, held it on ready. Tawney prowled the lounge. He glanced at the food on the table, then reached under the chair cushion and withdrew the disconnected microphone, looked at the loose wires, and tossed it aside.

"They're clean," the guard said.

Tawney's face was a study of uneasiness, but he clearly could not pinpoint what the trouble was. Finally he shrugged and turned on the smile again, although his eyes remained watchful. "Well, maybe you won't mind if I join in the talking for a while," he said. "You've been comfortable? No complaints?"

"No complaints," Greg said.

"Then I presume we're ready to talk business." He looked at Greg.

"You said you were ready to bargain," Greg said, "but I haven't heard any terms yet."

"Terms? Very simple. You direct us to the lode, we give you half of everything we realize from it," Tawney said, smiling.

"You mean you'll write us a contract? With a U.N. witness to it?"

"Well, hardly, under the circumstances. I'm afraid you'll have to take our word."

Greg looked at the company man and shook his head. "Not that I don't trust you," he said, "but I'm afraid I can't give you what you want."

"Why not?"

"Because I don't know where Dad made his strike."

The company man's face darkened. "Somebody knows

where it is. Your father would never have found something like that without telling his own sons."

"Sorry," Greg said. "Of course, I can tell you where you might find out, if you want to go look."

"We've already searched his records."

"*Some* of his records," Greg said. "Not all of them. There was a compartment behind the main control panel in Dad's orbit ship. Dad used it to store deeds, claims, and other important papers. There was a packet of notes in there before your men fired on the ship. But, of course, maybe you searched more thoroughly, the second time."

Tawney stared at him for a moment, then turned to Johnny. Johnny shrugged his shoulders solemnly and shook his head. Without a word, the little company man walked to the intercom speaker on the wall. He spoke sharply into it, waited, then had a brief, pungent conversation with someone. Then he turned back to Greg, his face heavy with suspicion. "You saw these papers?"

"Certainly I saw them. I didn't have time to read them through, but what else could they be?"

"Let me warn you," Tawney said coldly. "If I send a crew out there on a wild goose chase, the party will be over when they get back, do you understand? You've been given every consideration. If this is a fool's errand, you'll pay for it very dearly." He turned on his heel, snarled at one of the guards, "I want them watched every minute. One of you stay with them constantly. It won't take long to find out if this is a stall."

He stalked out, and the hatchway clanged behind him. One guard went along; the big one with the stunner stayed behind, eyeing his prisoners unpleasantly. The stunner was in his hand, the safety off.

Johnny Coombs started across the room toward the kitch-
enette, passing close to the guard. Suddenly he turned,
swung his fist heavily down on the guard's neck. The stunner
crackled, but Greg had jumped aside. Another blow from
Johnny's fist sent the gun flying. Another blow, and the
guard's legs slid out from under him. He fell unconscious
to the floor.

In an instant they were across the room, lifting down the
grill, helping Tom out of his hiding place. "Okay, boy,"
Johnny said to Greg, "I guess you pulled the trigger with
that story of yours."

"Not me," Greg said. "Tom did. He's the one that showed
us the way out—the same way he came in."

The guard would be out for a while, they made sure of that
first. Then there was a hasty consultation. "The airlocks are
guarded," Johnny said, "and if they tumble on to the ventilator shafts, they can smoke us out in no time. How are we
going to get a scout ship without showing ourselves? For that
matter, how are we going to get a scout ship away from here
without being blown up the way the *Scavenger* was blown
up?"

"I think I know a way," Tom said. "We have to have something to keep a lot of the crew busy. If we could get to the
ship's generators and put them out of commission somehow,
it might do it."

"Why?" Greg wanted to know.

"Because of the air supply," Tom said. "Without the generators, the fans won't run. They'll have to get a crew to fix
them or they'll suffocate."

"But that would only take a few men," Johnny said. "As
soon as the generators went out, they'd look for us, and if we

were missing, well, they'd have a whole crew beatin' the bushes for us. It wouldn't be long before somebody thought of the ventilators."

"But we've got to do something, and do it fast," Tom said.

"I know." Johnny chewed his lip. "It's a good idea, but we need more than just the generators. We've got to disable the ship, throw so many things at them so fast from so many different directions that they won't know which way to turn. That means we'll need to split up, and we'll need weapons." He hefted the guard's Markheim. "One stunner for the three of us isn't enough."

"Well, we have this." Tom unbuckled the gun case from his belt. "Dad's revolver. It's not a stunner, but it might help." He tossed the case to Johnny. "I can give you both a rundown on how the shafts go. We could plan to meet at a certain spot in a certain length of time—"

He broke off, looking at Johnny. The big miner had taken Roger Hunter's gun from the case and hefted it in his hand, starting to check it automatically as Tom talked. But now his hand froze as he stared at the weapon.

"What's wrong?" Tom asked.

"This gun is wrong," Johnny said. "All wrong. Where did you get this thing?"

"From Dad's spacer pack, the one the patrol brought back. The major gave it to us in Sun Lake City." Tom peered at the gun. "Is it broken or something? It's just Dad's revolver."

"It is, eh?" Johnny turned the gun over in his hand. "Who ever told you about guns?"

"What's wrong with it?"

There was an odd expression on Johnny's face as he handed the weapon back to Tom. "Take a look at it," he said. "Tell me whether it's loaded or not."

Tom looked at it. Except for a few hours on the firing range, he had had no experience with guns; he couldn't have taken apart a Markheim and reassembled it if his life depended on it. But he had seen his father take the old revolver out of the leather case many times before.

Now Tom could see that this was not the same gun.

The thing in his hand was large and awkward. The handgrips didn't fit; there was no trigger guard, and no trigger. Several inches along the gleaming metal barrel was a shiny stud, and below it a dial with notches on it.

"That's funny," Tom said. "I've never seen anything like this thing before."

Greg took it from him, balanced it in his hand. "Doesn't feel right," he said. "All out of balance."

"Look at the barrel," Johnny said quietly.

Greg looked. There was no hole in the end of the barrel. "This thing's crazy," he said.

"And then some," Johnny said. "You haven't had this out of the case since you took it from the pack?"

"Just once," said Tom, "and I put it right back. I hardly looked at it. Say, maybe it's just a new model Dad got."

"It's no new model. I'm not even sure it's a gun," Johnny said. "Doesn't *feel* like a gun."

"What happens when you push the stud here?" Greg asked.

Johnny licked his lips nervously. "Try it," he said.

Greg leveled the thing at the rear wall of the lounge and pressed the stud. There was a sharp buzzing sound, and a blinding flash of blue light against the wall. It looked for all the world like the flash of a live power line shorting out. They squinted at the flash, rubbed their eyes, and stared at the wall—or at what was left of the wall, because most of the wall was gone. The metal had bellied out in a six-foot hole into the storage hold beyond.

Johnny whistled. "This thing did *that?*" he whispered.

"It must have."

"But there's no gun ever made that could do that." He walked over to the hole in the wall. "That's half-inch steel plate. There's no way to pack that kind of energy into a hand gun."

They stared at the innocent-looking weapon in Greg's hand. "Whatever it is, Dad must have put it in the gun case."

"Yes, he must have," Johnny said.

"Well, don't you see what that means? *Dad must have found it somewhere.* Somewhere out here in the belt—a gun that no man could have made."

Tom took the weapon, ran his finger along the gleaming barrel. "I wonder," he said, "what else Dad found."

Somewhere below them they heard a hatch clang shut, and even deeper in the ship generator motors began throbbing in a steady even rhythm. In the silence of the lounge they could hear their own breathing, and outside, a thousand tiny sounds of the ship's activity were audible.

But now the only things that claimed their attention were the odd-shaped piece of metal in Greg's hand and the hole that gaped in the wall.

"You think that *this* was what Dad found?" Greg said. "The big strike he told Johnny about?"

"It must be part of it," Tom said.

"But what is it? And where did it come from? It doesn't make sense," Greg protested.

"It doesn't make sense the way we've been looking at it," Tom said. "All we've found was some gobbledegook in Dad's private log to tell us what he found. But it couldn't have been a vein of ore, or Tawney's men would have unearthed it. It had to be something else. Something that was so big and important that Dad didn't even dare let Johnny in on it."

"Yes, that's been the craziest part of it, to me," Johnny said. "I've done a lot of mining with your Dad. If he'd hit rich ore, he would have taken me out there to mine it with him. But he didn't. He said it was something he had to work alone for a while, and he sent me back."

"As if he'd found something that scared him," Tom said, "or something that he didn't understand. He was *afraid* to tell anybody. And whatever he found, he managed to hide it somewhere, so that nobody would find it."

"Then why didn't he hide this part of it, too?" Greg said.

"Maybe to be sure there was some trace left, if anything happened to him," Tom said.

They were silent for a moment. The only sound was the stertorous breathing of the unconscious guard. "Well," Greg said finally, "I have to admit it makes sense. It makes other things add up better, too. Dad was no fool, he must have known that Tawney was onto something. And Dad would never have risked his life for an ore strike. He'd either have made a deal with Tawney or let him hijack the lode, if that was all there was to it. But there's still one big question. Where did he hide what he found? We aren't going to find the answer here, that's certain." He walked over to the hole in the wall.

"Made quite a mess of it, didn't it?" Johnny said.

"Looks like it. I wonder what that thing would do to a ship's generator plant." He turned to Johnny. "We haven't much time. With this thing, we could tear this ship apart, leave them so confused they'll never know what broke loose.

And if we could get this gun back to Major Briarton, he'd have to listen to us, and get the U.N. patrol into the search."

They had been so intent on their conversation that they did not hear the footsteps in the corridor until the door swung open. It was another guard, the one who had departed with Tawney. He stopped short, blinking at his companion on the floor and at the gaping hole in the wall. A strangled sound came from his throat.

Johnny grabbed his arm, jerked him into the lounge, and slammed the hatch shut. Greg pulled the stunner from his holster and tossed it to Tom. The guard let out a roar, twisted free, and met Johnny's fist as he came around. He sagged at the knees and slid to the floor beside the other guard. "All right," Johnny said, "we've dealt the cards, now we'd better play the hand. Tom, you first."

Tom pulled the ventilator grill down and climbed up into the shaft. Greg followed, with Johnny at his heels, pulling the grill back up into place from the inside. They waited for a moment, but there was no sound from the lounge.

"All right," Johnny said breathlessly. "Let's move."

Swiftly they started down the dark tunnel.

*Chapter Eleven*

---

## THE HAUNTED SHIP

THEY did not pause, even to catch their breath, for the first twenty minutes as Tom led them swiftly and silently through the maze of corridors and chutes that made up the ventilation system of the huge ship. Greg lost his bearings completely in the first twenty seconds; each time his brother paused at a junction of tubes, he felt a wave of panic rise up in his throat. Suppose they lost themselves in here! He heard Johnny's trousers flapping behind him, saw Tom's figure flit past another grill up ahead, and plunged doggedly on.

It was amazingly hard to move quietly. Even in stocking feet they made a soft thud with each footfall. In the darkness their breathing was magnified a thousandfold. It seemed incredible that they did not sound like steam engines chugging past each compartment grill.

But there was no sign of detection, no sound of alarm. Finally they came out into a large shaft which allowed them to stand upright. They stopped to catch their breath.

"Main tube to the living quarters," Tom said when they caught up with him. "Joins with the lower level tube by a series of chutes. We've actually been circumnavigating the ship. I wanted to get as far away from that lounge compartment as possible, in case they check up on you right away."

"We can't have much time," Johnny said. "That second guard must have been comin' to relieve the other, and when the first one doesn't report back, they'll smell somethin' fishy."

They talked it over for a moment. Johnny had been careful to leave the hatchway into the corridor ajar before he climbed into the ventilator shaft, and then he had pulled the shaft snugly into place behind him. Anyone who came would find two unconscious guards, a burnt-out hole in the wall, and the door unlocked.

"Let's hope that whoever gets to the lounge first will take things at face value and assume we're at large in the ship somewhere, for a while at least," Johnny said. "That hole in the wall is going to slow them up a bit too."

"But they'll sound the alarm," Tom said.

"You bet they will! They'll have every man on the crew shakin' down the ship for us. But they may not think of the ventilators until they can't find us anywhere else."

"But sooner or later they're bound to think of it."

"That's true," Johnny said. "Unless they keep seein' us in the ship. The way I figure it, this crew has been on battle stations plenty of times. They'll be able to search the whole ship in half an hour. We're just goin' to have to show ourselves—at least enough to keep them searchin'."

"Well, what if they do think of the ventilators?" Greg asked. "They'd still have a time finding us."

"Maybe, but don't underestimate Tawney. He might mask up his crew and flood the tubes with cyanide."

They thought about that for a minute. There was no sound but their own breathing, and the low *chug-chug-chug* of the pumps somewhere deep in the ship. Momentarily they expected to hear the raucous clang of the alarm bell, as some crew member or another walked into the lounge and found them gone. But so far there was no sign that they had been discovered missing.

"No," Johnny said finally, "if we just hide out in here, and hope for a chance at one of the scout ships, they'll find us eventually. But we've got three big advantages, if we can figure out how to use them. That fancy gun, for one. A way to get around the ship, for another. And the fact that there's one more of us than they count on." He flipped on his pocket flash and began to draw lines on the dusty floor of the shaft. "My idea is to keep them so busy fightin' little fires that they won't have a chance to worry about where the big one is."

He drew a rough outline sketch of the organization of the ship. "This look right to you, from what you've seen?" he asked Tom.

"Pretty much," Tom said. "There are more connecting tubes."

"All the better. We want to get the generators with our little toy here first. That'll darken the ship and put the blowers out of commission in case they think of using gas. Also, it will cut out their computers and missile launching rigs, which might give us a chance to get a scout ship away in one piece if we could get aboard one."

"All right, the generators are first," Tom said. "But then what? There are four hundred men on this ship. They'll have every airlock triple guarded."

"Not when we get through, they won't," Johnny grinned. "We've got an old friend aboard who's going to help us."

"*Friend?*"

"Ever hear of panic?" Johnny said. "Just listen a minute."

Quickly he outlined his plan. Tom and Greg listened carefully, watching Johnny make marks with his finger in the dust. When he finished, Greg whistled softly. "You missed your life work," he said. "You should have gone into crime."

"If I'd had a ghost to help me, I might have," Johnny said.

"It's perfect," Tom said, "if it works. But it all depends on one thing—keeping things rolling after we start."

For another five minutes they went over the details. Then Johnny clapped them each on the shoulder. "It's up to you two," he said. "Let's go."

The three moved down the large shaft to the place where it broke into several spurs. Johnny started down the chute toward the engine rooms; Tom and Greg headed in opposite directions toward the main body of the ship. Just as they broke up, they heard a muffled metallic sound from the nearest compartment grill.

It was the *clang-clang-clang* of the orbit ship's general alarm.


Merrill Tawney had not noticed the first guard's failure to report back for almost half an hour after the second guard had been dispatched. Then he had glanced angrily at the wall clock, and rang the lounge. There was no answer. Another guard was summoned and told to head for the nearest shuttle car. He found the hatchway standing ajar, with the two guards on the floor, just groggily coming around.

Something had hit them, but neither was quite sure what.

The guard took one look at the hole burned in the wall, and ran to the wall phone in the corridor.

"They're gone," he panted when he finally reached Tawney in control cabin. "Must have jumped the guards. Got their stunners, and—" he hesitated, then told Tawney about the wall.

"What do you mean, blew a hole through it?" Tawney snarled.

"I swear that's what they did, boss, six feet across."

"You mean a blowtorch?"

"Doesn't look like a torch. I never saw anything like it."

"Well, get a crew in there," Tawney said. "Seal off every corridor in the area, and search every compartment. They can't hide on this ship, stunners or no stunners."

Tawney waited, seething, until the first reports began coming in. All the corridors in the quadrant were sealed. Guard crews went through them from both ends, meeting in the middle. Every compartment in the quadrant had been searched and then locked.

But there was no sign of the fugitives.

Moments later the general alarm bell went off, beating its reverberating tattoo in every compartment on the ship. Crewmen stopped with food halfway to their mouths, jerked away from tables. Orders buzzed along a dozen wires, and section chiefs began reporting their battle stations alert and ready. Finally Tawney snapped on the general public address system speaker. "Now get this," he roared. "I want every inch of this ship searched—every corridor, every compartment. I want a special crew standing by for missile launching. I want double guards at every airlock. If they get a ship away from here, the man who lets them through had better be dead when I find him." He broke off, clutching the speaker until his voice was under control again. "All right, move. They're armed, but there's no place they can go. Find them."

A section chief came back over the speaker. "Dead or alive, boss?"

"Alive, you idiot! At least the Hunter brat. I'll take the other one any way you can get him."

He switched off, and waited, pacing the control cabin like a caged animal. Ten minutes later a buzzer sounded. "Hydroponics, boss. All clear."

"No sign of them?"

"Nothing."

Another buzz. "Number Seven ore hold. Nothing here."

Still another buzz. "Crew's quarters. Nothing, boss."

One by one the reports came in. Fuming, Tawney checked off the sections, watched the net draw tighter throughout the ship. They were somewhere, they *had* to be.

But nobody seemed to find them.

He was buzzing for his first mate when the power went off. The lights went out, the speaker went dead in his hand. The computers sighed contentedly and stopped computing. Abruptly, the emergency circuits went into operation, flooding the darkness with harsh white light. The intercom started buzzing again.

"Engine room, boss."

"What happened down there?" Tawney roared.

The man sounded as if he'd just run the mile. "Generators," he panted. "Blown out."

"Well, get somebody in there to fix them. Have a crew seal off the area."

"Can't, boss. Fix them, I mean."

"Why not?" What have we got electricians for?"

"There's nothing left to fix. The generators aren't wrecked. They're demolished."

"Then get the pair that did it."

"They're not here. We've been sealed up tight. There's no way anybody could have gotten in here."

After that, things really began to get confusing!

For a while Merrill Tawney thought his crew was going crazy. Then he began to wonder if he were the one who was losing his mind.

Whatever the case, Merrill Tawney was certain of one thing. The things that were happening on his orbit ship could not possibly be happening.

A guard in one of the outer-shell storage holds called in with a disquieting report. Greg Hunter, it seemed, had just been spotted vanishing into one of the storage compartments from the main outer-shell corridor. When the guard had broken through the jammed hatchway to collar his trapped victim, there was no sign of the victim anywhere around.

At the same moment, a report came in from a guard on the opposite side of the ship. He had just spotted Greg Hunter *there*, it seemed, moving down a spur corridor. The guard had held his fire (according to Tawney's orders) and summoned help to corner the quarry, but when help arrived, the quarry had vanished.

Five minutes later the Hunter boy was discovered in the hydroponics section, busily reducing all the yeast vats to shambles with a curious weapon that seemed to eat holes in things. It ate the deck out from under the guard's feet, sending him plunging through the floor into the galley. By the time he had scrambled back again, the Hunter boy was gone, and a rapid move to seal off the region failed to turn him up again.

The guard was upset. Tawney was a great deal more upset, because at the time Greg Hunter was (reportedly) playing havoc with the yeast vats in Hydroponics he was also (reportedly) knocking guards down like tenpins in the main corridor off the engine room while reinforcements tried to pin him down with a wide-beam stunner.

Suddenly emergency circuits closed and lights flashed in the control cabin, the special signal for a meteor collision with the outer shell in #3 hold. Tawney signaled frantically for the section chief. "What's happening down there?"

"I can't talk," the section chief gasped. "Gotta get into a suit, we're leaking air in here."

"Well, plug up the hole!"

"The hole's four feet wide, sir!" There was a fit of coughing and the contact broke. The signals for #4 hold and #5 hold were flashing now. While crew members in the vicinity scrambled for pressure suits, someone systematically proceeded to blow holes in #9, #10, and #11 holds.

It was impossible, but the reports came in thick and fast. Greg Hunter was in two places at once, and everywhere he went in both places he left a trail of unbelievable destruction —bulkheads demolished, gaping holes torn in the outer shell, the air-reconditioning units smashed beyond repair. Tawney buzzed for his first mate.

An emergency switch cut into the line. The frantic voice of a section chief reported that Johnny Coombs had been spotted disappearing into a ventilator shaft in the engine sector. "Go in after him!" Tawney screamed. He got his first mate finally, and snarled orders into the speaker. "They're in the ventilators. Get a crew in there and stop them."

But it was dark in the ventilator shafts. No emergency lights in there. Worse, the crewmen were hearing the rumors that were being whispered around the ship. The ventilator shafts yawned menacingly before them; they went in reluctantly. Once in the dark maze of tunnels, identification was difficult. Two guards met each other headlong in the darkness, and put each other out of the fight in a flurry of nervous stunner fire. While others searched, more of the holds were broken open, leaking air through gaping rents in the hull.

Tawney felt the panic spreading; he tried to curb it, but it spread in spite of him. The fugitives were appearing and disappearing like wraiths. Reports back to control cabin took on a hysterical note, confused and garbled. Now the second-level bulkheads were being attacked. Over a third of the compartments were leaking precious air into outer space.

When a terrified section chief came through with a report that two Greg Hunters had been spotted by the same man at the same time, and that the guards in the sector were shooting at anything that moved, including other guards, Tawney made his way to the radio cabin and put through a frantic signal to Jupiter Equilateral headquarters on Mars.

The contact took forever, even with the ship's powerful emergency boosters. By the time someone at headquarters was reading him, Tawney's report made little sense. He was trying for the third time to explain, clearly and logically, how two men and a ghost were scuttling his orbit ship under his very feet when one wall of the cabin vanished in a crackle of blue fire, and he found himself staring at two Greg Hunters and a grim-faced Johnny Coombs.

He made squeaky noises into the microphone and dropped it with a crash. He groped for a chair; Johnny jerked him to his feet again. "A scout ship," he said tersely. "Clear it for launchin'. We want one with plenty of fuel, and we don't want a single guard anywhere near the airlock." He picked up an intercom microphone and thrust it into the little fat man's trembling hand. "Now move! And you'd better be sure they understand you, because you're comin' with us."

Merrill Tawney stared first at Tom, then at Greg, and finally at the microphone. Then he moved. The orders he gave to his section chiefs were very clear.

He had never argued with a ghost before, and he didn't care to start now.

It was over so quickly that it seemed to Tom it had just begun, and if so much had not been at stake, it might have been fun.

It was the gun—the remarkable gun that Roger Hunter had left as his legacy—that was the key. It ate through steel and aluminum alloy like putty. Whatever its source of power, however it worked, by whatever means it had been built, there had been no match for it on the orbit ship.

It had *worked*, and that was all that mattered right then. With it, and with the advantage of a ghost that walked like a man—Tom Hunter, to be exact—they reduced the Jupiter Equilateral orbit ship to a smoking wreck in something less than thirty minutes.

The signal came back that a scout ship was ready, unguarded. Johnny prodded Tawney with the stunner. "You first," he said.

"Where are you taking me?"

"You'll see," Johnny said.

"It was a trick," Tawney said, glaring at Tom. "They told me they shot your ship to pieces."

"The ship, yes," Tom said. "Not me."

"Well—well, that's good, that's good," Tawney said quickly.

He turned to Greg. "You don't have to take me back. Our bargain is still good."

"Move," Johnny Coombs said.

With Tawney between them, Greg and Tom marched down the corridor toward the airlock, Johnny bringing up the rear. No one stopped them. No one even came near them. One crewman stumbled on them in the corridor. He saw Tawney with a gun in his back and fled in terror.

They found the scout ship, and strapped Tawney down to an acceleration bunk, binding his hands and feet so he couldn't move. Greg checked the controls while Tom and Johnny strapped down. A moment later the engines fired, and the leaking wreck of the orbit ship fell away, dwindling and disappearing in the blackness of space.

It was a quiet journey. The red dot that was Mars grew larger every hour. One of the three stayed awake at all times to watch Tawney while the others slept. In the second rest period, Tom woke up to find Greg peering toward Mars with the view screen on telescopic.

"Looking for a German band to welcome us home?"

Greg grinned and leaned back, rubbing his eyes. "No, just looking. I thought I could see the Star-Jump satellite for a minute, but I guess not."

"You wish you were back there, I suppose."

Greg thought about it, and nodded his head. "It's what I want to do. Someday the men at Star-Jump will be the ones that make the long trip out. Probably Alpha Centauri first, that's closest. Then Sirius, Vega, Altair, Arcturus—" He nodded again. "The ones that will go will be the lucky ones."

"Or the crazy ones," Tom said.

Greg laughed. "Maybe crazy, too, I don't know. But somebody *has* to find the way to go." He stood up, snapped off the view screen. "I'd like to be back there, sure, but right now I've a more important job."

"How's our prisoner doing?"

"No problem there, he can barely move. I almost wish he'd try something, he's too quiet."

It was true. Tawney had recovered from his shock, but rather than grow more worried as Mars grew larger on the screen, he seemed to become more cheerful by the minute. "He doesn't seem very worried, does he?" Tom said.

"No, and it doesn't quite add up. We've got enough on him to get Jupiter Equilateral pushed right out of the belt."

They mentioned it to Johnny later. "Almost as though he had something up his sleeve," Greg said.

Johnny chewed his lip thoughtfully. "His company has plenty of power on Mars. But with the three of us to testify, I don't see how he has a chance."

"I'd still feel better if we had the whole picture for the major," Tom said. "We still don't know what Dad found, or where he hid it."

They slept on it, but the uneasiness grew. Tawney ignored them, staring at the image of the red planet on the view screen almost eagerly. Then, eight hours out of Sun Lake City a U.N. patrol ship appeared, moving toward them swiftly. "Intercepting orbit," Greg said. "Looks like they were waiting for us."

They watched as the big ship moved in to tangential orbit, matching its speed to theirs. Then Greg snapped the communicator switch. "Sound off," he said cheerfully. "We've got a prize for you."

"Stand by, we're boarding you," the patrol sent back. "And put your weapons aside."

Four scooters broke from the side of the patrol ship. Greg

activated the airlock. Five minutes later a man in patrol uniform with captain's bars stepped into the control cabin, a stunner on ready in his hand. Three patrolmen came in behind him.

The captain looked around the cabin, saw Tawney, and took a deep breath. "Well, thank the stars you're safe at any rate. Pete, Jimmy, take the controls."

"Hold on," Greg said. "We don't need a pilot."

The captain looked at him. "Sorry, but we're taking you in. There won't be any trouble unless you make it. You three are under arrest, and I'm authorized to make it stick if I have to."

They stared at him. Then Johnny said, "What are the charges?"

"You ought to know," the captain said. "We have a formal complaint from the main offices of Jupiter Equilateral, charging you with piracy, murder, kidnaping of a company official, and totally wrecking a company orbit ship. I don't quite see how you managed it, but we're going to find out in short order."

There was a stunned silence in the cabin, and then a sound came from the rear of the cabin that made the three of them turn.

Merrill Tawney was laughing.

# Chapter Twelve

## THE RAZOR'S EDGE

THE room was small and drab, lit only by pale afternoon sunlight filtering in through the tiny windows. Tom had seen the internment rooms at the Sun Lake City space port before from the outside; from the inside, with the heavy door closed and bolted, things looked very much different. It seemed like hours since the captain had escorted them down the long corridor into the room. Actually only twenty minutes had crept by on the wall clock. They stared through the windows at the failing sunlight, and wondered what was delaying the major.

Outside, the port was humming with activity. One of the great Jupiter Equilateral freighters had just finished loading its holds with a cargo of finished vanadium steel milling tools, bound for a dozen factories on Earth. The gantry cranes which had lifted the cartons into the afterholds of the ship were being moved away now, and preparations for blast-off began. At midnight, Mars time, one of the Earth-Mars orbit ships would reach its point of closest apposition to Mars.

The freighter would be there to meet her, to unload the precious cargo for its long run to Earth.

Now a crew of power-pile men in their bright yellow uniforms went aboard to complete their check-over of the engines, to make certain that the fusion reaction that powered the freighter would develop the necessary thrust to lift it and its cargo against Mars' gravitational pull, and to make sure too that those engines would cut off at the proper time. Still another crew moved around the perimeter of the radiation screen, ready with radiation detecting apparatus to make sure that none of the furiously radioactive backwash from the engines escaped from the tight circle of the damping screen to contaminate the surrounding field and buildings.

It was all very businesslike and efficient. Tom thought gloomily as he watched. Sun Lake City, Mars, was coming into its own as a city, not as a city of Earth, but as a city of the solar system. For a hundred years the Mars colonies had cost Earth-side taxpayers billions of dollars for their support. The cost of just establishing those colonies had been fantastic; it had cost even more to keep them going, to provide food and machinery and living space for the men and women who had come here.

But now, slowly, the tables were turning. An economy was developing on Mars, a mining economy. Like Alaska in the early days of its statehood, Mars had struggled to produce more than it cost, and now it was winning the struggle. Mars was beginning now to pay its own way, and more.

And in the future, what would Mars become? A place for the overflow of population from the huge Earth cities? A place to provide homes and work and a way of life for millions of humans who would soon have no place on Earth?

Perhaps. Tom thought of his one short visit to Earth, the

last vacation trip his family had taken before the sickness came. He remembered the mammoth crowded city they had visited, stretching from Boston Sector in the north down to Richmond Sector in the south, and west almost to the borders of Greater Pittsburgh—one huge, teeming city rising in skyscrapers almost to the sky, and digging deep into the ground. It had been an exciting place to see, but he knew now that it was only one of the sprawling cities that covered the Earth.

It was not a problem of enough food, or enough work—it was a problem of standing room. Another hundred years, and Earth would be bursting at the seams. Even the most optimistic dreamers knew that when that time came, even Mars would not be enough. Mars and Venus together would not be enough. Even if the planetary engineers succeeded in turning Mars into a habitable planet for humans not requiring bubble-enclosed cities; even if they could change Venus from a poisonous hot-box into a warm tropical planet with plenty of oxygen and water, it would not be enough.

Tom turned away from the window, and looked up at the wall clock. How many people were born on Earth every minute? Greg was right when he said that Project Star-Jump was the only hope. The new land in the Amazon, in Greenland and Antarctica had been swallowed up in two decades. Mars and Venus would be swallowed up in a hundred years. The stars would have to be next. A place for men to escape. . . .

The thought of escape brought him back sharply. Half an hour now, and still no word from the major. From the moment the patrol crew had boarded them, everything had seemed like a bad dream. The shock of the arrest, the realization that the captain had been serious when he reeled off the charges lodged against them—they had been certain it was some kind of ill-planned joke until they saw the delegation of Jupiter Equilateral officials waiting at the port to greet Merrill Tawney like a man returned from the dead. They watched Tawney climb into the sleek company car and drive off toward the gate, while the captain escorted them without a word to the internment room.

True, they had not been stripped of their clothes and held under guard. No one had touched them. In fact, no one had spoken to them, or paid any attention to their protests. The U.N. officer at the desk checked their ID's, jotted a note on the pad in front of him, and flipped the speaker switch to contact Major Briarton.

And now, angry and shaken, they were staring through the windows and waiting.

The door clicked, and the captain looked in. "All right, come along now," he said.

"Is the major here?" Tom asked.

"You'll see the major soon enough." The captain herded them into another room, where a clerk efficiently finger-printed them. Then they went down a ramp to a jitney platform, and boarded a U.N. official car. The trip into the city was slow; rush-hour traffic from the port was heavy. When they reached U.N. headquarters, there was another wait in an upper level anteroom. The captain stood stiffly with his hands behind his back and ignored them.

"Look, this is ridiculous," Greg burst out finally. "We haven't done anything. You haven't even let us make a statement."

"Make your statement to the major. It's his headache, not mine, I'm happy to say."

"But you let that man walk out of there scot free."

The captain looked at him. "If I were you," he said, "I'd stop complaining and start worrying. If I had Jupiter Equilateral at my throat, I'd worry plenty, because once they start they don't stop."

A signal light blinked and he took them downstairs. Major Briarton was behind his desk, his eyes tired, his face grim. He dismissed the captain, and motioned them to seats. "All right, let's have the story," he said, "and by the ten moons of Saturn it had better be convincing, because I've about had my fill of you three."

He listened without interruption as Tom told the story, with Greg and Johnny adding details from time to time. Tom told him everything, from the moment they had blasted off for Roger Hunter's claim to the moment the patrol ship had boarded them, except for a single detail. He didn't mention the remarkable gun from Roger Hunter's gun case. The gun was still in the spacer's pack he had slung over his shoulder; he had not mentioned it when the patrolmen had taken their stunners away. Now as he talked, he felt a twinge of guilt in not mentioning it.

But he had a reason. Dad had died to keep the gun a secret. It seemed only right to keep the secret a little longer. When he came to the part about their weapons, he simply spoke of "Dad's gun" and omitted any details. All through the story, the major listened intently, interrupting only occasionally, pulling at his lip and scowling.

"So we decided that the best way to convince you that we had the evidence you wanted was to bring Tawney back with us," Tom concluded.

"A brilliant maneuver," the major said dryly. "A real stroke of genius."

"But then the patrol ship intercepted us and told us we

were under arrest. And when we landed, they let Tawney drive off without even questioning him."

"The least they could do, under the circumstances," the major said.

"Well, I'd like to know why," Greg broke in bitterly. "Why pick on us? We've just been telling you—"

"Yes, yes, I heard every word of it," the major sighed. "If you knew the trouble—oh, what's the use? I've spent the last three solid hours talking myself hoarse, throwing in every bit of authority I could muster and jeopardizing my position as co-ordinator here, for the sole purpose of keeping you three idiots out of jail for a few hours."

"Jail!"

"That's what I said. The brig. The place they put people when they don't behave. You three are sitting on a nice, big powder keg right now, and when it blows I don't know how much of you is going to be left."

"Do you think we're lying?" Greg asked.

"Do you know what you're charged with?" the major snapped back.

"Some sort of nonsense about piracy."

"Plus kidnaping. Plus murder. To say nothing of totally disabling a seventeen-million-dollar orbit ship and placing the lives of four hundred crewmen in jeopardy." The major picked up a sheet of paper from his desk. "According to Merrill Tawney's statement, the three of you hijacked a company scout ship that chanced to be scouting in the vicinity of your father's claim. Your attack was unprovoked and violent. Everybody on Mars knows you were convinced that Jupiter Equilateral was responsible for your father's death." He looked up. "In the absence of any evidence, I might add, although I did my best to tell you that." He rattled the report sheet. "All right. You took the scout ship by force, with the pilot at gunpoint, and made him home in on his orbit ship. Then you proceeded to reduce that orbit ship to a leaking wreck, although Tawney tried to reason with you and even offered you amnesty if you would desist. By the time the crew stopped shooting each other in the dark— fifteen of them subsequently expired, it says here—you had stolen another scout ship and kidnaped Tawney for the purpose of extorting a confession out of Jupiter Equilateral, threatening him with torture if he did not comply." The major dropped the paper on the desk.

Johnny Coombs picked it up, looked at it owlishly, and put it back again. "Pretty large operation for three men, Major," he said.

The major shrugged. "You were armed. That orbit ship was registered as a commercial vessel. It had no reason to expect a surprise attack and had no way to defend itself."

"They were armed to the teeth," Greg said disgustedly. "Why don't you send somebody out to look?"

"Oh, I could, but why waste the time and fuel? There wouldn't be any weapons aboard."

"Then how do they explain the fact that the *Scavenger* was blown to bits and Dad's orbit ship ripped apart from top to bottom?"

"Details," the major said. "Mere details. I'm sure that the company's lawyers can muddy the waters quite enough so that little details like that are overlooked. Particularly with a sympathetic jury and a judge that plays along."

He stood up and ran his hand through his hair. "All right, granted I'm painting the worst picture possible, but I'm afraid that's the way it's going to be. I believe your story, don't worry about that. I know why you went out there to the belt and I can't really blame you, I suppose. But you were asking for trouble, and that's what you got. Frankly, I am amazed that you ever returned to Mars, and how you managed to make rubble of an orbit ship with a crew of four hundred men trying to stop you is more than I can comprehend. But you did it. All right, fine. You were justified; they attacked you, held you prisoner, threatened you. Fine. They'd have cut your throats in another few hours, perhaps. Fine. I believe you. But there's one big question that you can't answer, and unless you can no court in the solar system will listen to you."

"What question?" Tom said.

"The question of motives," the major replied. "You had plenty of motive for doing what Tawney says you did. But what motive did Jupiter Equilateral have, if your story is true?"

"They wanted to get what Dad found, out in the belt."

"Ah, yes, that mysterious bonanza that Roger Hunter found. I was afraid that was what you'd say. And it's the reason that Jupiter Equilateral is going to win this fight, and you're going to lose it."

"I don't think I understand," Tom said slowly.

"I mean that I'm going to have to testify against you," the major said. *"Because your father didn't find a thing in the Asteroid Belt,* and I happen to know it."

"It's been a war," the major said later, "a dirty vicious war with no holds barred and no quarter given. Not a shooting war, of course, nothing out in the open, but a war just the same, with the highest stakes of any war in history."

It was late; the office staff in the co-ordinator's suite had gone home. On the streets of the city there was a momentary lull as the colonists rested from the day's work, and prepared for the evening activities.

"It didn't look like a war, at first," the major went on. "Back when the colonies were being built, nobody really believed that anything of value would come of them, scientific outposts, perhaps, places for laboratories and observatories, not much more. The colonies were placed under United Nations control. Nobody argued about it.

"And then things began to change. There was wealth out here and opportunities for power. With the overpopulation at home, Earth was looking more and more to Mars and Venus for a place to move, not tiny colonies, but places for millions of people. And as Mars grew, Jupiter Equilateral grew."

"But it was just a mining company," Tom said.

"At first it was, but then its interests began to expand. The company accumulated wealth, unbelievable wealth, and it developed many friends. Very soon it had friends back on Earth fighting for it, and the United Nations found itself fighting to stay on Mars."

"I don't see why," Tom said. "The company already has half the mining claims in the belt."

"They aren't interested in the mining," the major said. "They have a much longer-range goal than that. The men behind Jupiter Equilateral are looking ahead. They know that some day Earthmen are going to have to go to the stars for colonies. It won't be a matter of choice after a while; they'll *have* to go. Well, Jupiter Equilateral's terms are very simple. They're perfectly willing to let the United Nations control things on Earth. All they want is control of everything else. Mars, if they can drive us out. Venus too, if it ever proves suitable for colonization. If they can gain control of the ships that leave our solar system for the stars, they can build an empire, and they know it."

They were silent for a moment. Then Johnny Coombs said, "Doesn't anybody on Earth know about this?"

"There are some who know but they don't see the danger. They think of Jupiter Equilateral as just another big company. So far, U.N. control of Mars and Venus has held up, even though the pressure on the legislators back on Earth has been getting heavier and heavier. Jupiter Equilateral won the greatest fight in its history when they got U.N. jurisdiction limited to Mars, and kept us out of the belt. And now they hope to convince the lawmakers that we're incompetent to administer the Martian colonies and keep peace out here. If they succeed, we'll be called home in nothing flat; we've had to fight just to stay."

The major spread his hands helplessly. "As I said, it's been a war. Our only hope was to prove that the company was using piracy and murder to gain control of the asteroids. We had to find a way to smash the picture they've been painting of themselves back on Earth as a big, benevolent organization interested only in the best for Earth colonists on the planets. We had to expose them before they had the Earth in chains, not now, maybe not even a century from now, but sometime, years from now, when the break-through to the stars comes and Earthmen discover that if they want to leave Earth they have to pay a toll."

"They could never do that!" Greg protested.

"They're doing it, son. And they're winning. We have been searching desperately for a way to fight back, and that was where your father came in. He could see the handwriting on the wall, he knew what was happening. That was why he broke with the company and tried to organize a compet-

ing force before it was too late. And it was why he died in
the belt. He knew I couldn't send an agent out there without
unquestionable evidence of major crime of some sort or
another. But a private citizen could go out there, and if he
happened to be working with the U.N. hand in glove, nobody
could do anything about it."

"Then Dad was a U.N. agent?"

"Oh, not officially. There's not a word in the records. If I
were forced to testify under oath, I would have to deny any
connection. But unofficially, he went out there to lay a trap."

The major told them then. It had been an incredible risk
that Roger Hunter had taken, but the decision had been his.
The plan was simple: to involve Jupiter Equilateral in a
case of claim jumping and piracy that would hold up in
court, pressed by a man who would not be intimidated and
could not be bought out. Roger Hunter had made a trip to
the belt and come back with stories—very carefully planted
in just the right ears—of a fabulous strike. He knew that
Jupiter Equilateral had jumped a hundred rich claims in the
past, forcing the independent miners to agree, frightening
them into silence or disposing of them with "accidents."

But this was one claim they were not going to jump. The
U.N. co-operated, helping him spread the story of his big
strike until they were certain that Jupiter Equilateral would
go for the bait. Then Roger Hunter had returned to the belt,
with a U.N. patrol ship close by in case he needed help.

"We thought it would be enough," the major said un-
happily. "We were wrong, of course. At first nothing happened, not a sign of a company ship, nothing. Your father
contacted me finally. He was ready to give up. Somehow
they must have learned that it was a trap. But they were care-

ful. They waited until our guard was down, and then moved in fast and hit hard."

He sank down in his seat behind the desk, regarding the Hunter twins sadly. "You know the rest. Perhaps you can see now why I tried to keep you from going out there. There was no proof to uncover, and no bonanza lode for you to find. There never was a bonanza lode."

The twins looked at each other, and then at the major. "Why didn't you tell us?" Greg said.

"Would you have listened? Would telling you have kept you from going out there? There was no point to telling you, I knew you would have to find out for yourselves, however painfully. But what I'm telling you now is the truth."

"As far as it goes," Tom said. "But if this is really the truth, there's one thing that doesn't fit into the picture."

Slowly he pulled the gun case from his pack and set it down on the major's desk. "It doesn't explain what Dad was doing with this."

## Chapter Thirteen

### "...I WILL PUT A PLANET"

TOM knew now that it was the right thing to do. There was no question, after the major's story, of what Dad had been doing out in the belt at the time he had been killed. He had been doing a job that was more important to him than asteroid mining, but he had found something more important than his own life, and had no chance to send word of what he had found back to Major Briarton on Mars. That had been the unforeseeable part of the trap.

But now, of course, the major had to know.

The Mars co-ordinator looked at the thing on his desk for a long moment before he reached out to touch it. The bright metal gleamed in the light—pale gray, lustrous. The major picked it up, balanced it expertly in his hand, and a puzzled frown wrinkled his face. He examined it minutely.

"What is this thing?" he asked.

"Suppose you tell us," Johnny Coombs said from across the room.

"It looks like a gun."

"That's what it is, all right."

"You've fired it?"

"Yes, but I wouldn't fire it in here, if I were you," Johnny said. "You were wonderin' how we wrecked Tawney's orbit ship so thoroughly. That's your answer right there." He told about the hole in the bulkhead, the way the ship's generators had melted like clay under the powerful blast of the weapon.

The major could hardly control his excitement. "Where did you get it?" he asked, turning to Tom.

"From the space pack that you turned over to us. I didn't even look at it, until we needed a gun in a hurry. I just assumed it was Dad's revolver."

"Your father found it somewhere in the belt," the major said softly. He looked at the weapon again, shaking his head. "There couldn't be any such gun," he said finally. "The things you say it can do would require energy enough to break down the cohesive forces of molecules. There isn't any way we know of to harness that kind of energy and channel it in a hand weapon. Nobody on Earth—"

He broke off and stared at them.

"That's right," Johnny Coombs said quietly. "Nobody on Earth."

"You mean—extraterrestrial?"

"There isn't any other answer," Johnny said. "*Look* at the thing, Major. *Feel* it. Does it feel like it was made for a human hand? It doesn't fit, it doesn't balance, you have to hold it with both hands to aim it."

"*But where did it come from?*" the Major asked. "We've never had visitors from another star system, not in the course of recorded history. And we know that Earthmen are the only intelligent creatures in our solar system."

"You mean that they're the only ones *now*," Tom said.

"Or any other time."

"We don't know that, for sure," Tom said.

"Look, we've explored Venus, Mars, all the major satellites. If there had ever been any signs of intelligent beings on any of them, we'd have known it."

"Maybe there was a planet that Earthmen haven't explored," Tom said. "Dad tried to tell us that. The quotation from Kepler that he scribbled down in his log: 'Between Jupiter and Mars I will put a planet.' Why would Dad write that? Unless he suddenly discovered proof that there *had* been a planet there?"

"You mean this gun," the major said.

"And whatever else he found."

"But there's never been any proof of that theory, not even a hint of proof."

"Maybe Dad found proof. There are hundreds of thousands of asteroid fragments out there in the belt, and only a few hundred of them have ever been examined by men."

On the desk the strange weapon stared up at them. Evidence, mute evidence, and yet its very existence said more than a thousand words. It was there. It could not be denied.

And someone—or *something*—had made it.

Slowly the major pulled himself to his feet. "It must have happened after his last message to me," he said. "It wasn't part of the scheme we had set up, but he made a strike just the same, an archeological strike, and this gun was part of it." He picked up the weapon, turned it over in his hand. "But it was days after that last message before his signal went off, and the patrol ship moved in."

"It makes sense," Johnny Coombs said. "He found the gun, and somethin' more."

"Like what?"

"I wouldn't even guess," Johnny said. "A planet with a race of creatures intelligent enough and advanced enough to make a weapon like that—it could have been anything. But whatever it was, it must have scared him. He must have known that a company ship might turn up any minute, so he hid whatever he had found."

"And now it's vanished," the major said. "The big flaw in the whole idea. My patrol ship found nothing when it searched the region. You looked, and drew a blank. The company men scoured the area." He sighed. "You see, it just won't hold up, not a bit of it. Even with this gun, it won't hold up."

"It's out there somewhere," Tom said doggedly. "It's got to be."

"But *where?* Don't you see that everything hangs on that one thing? If we could prove that your father found something just before he was killed, we could tear Jupiter Equilateral's case against you to shreds. We could charge them with piracy and murder, and make it stick. We could break their power once and for all, but until we know what Roger Hunter found, we're helpless. They'll take you three to court, and I won't be able to stop them. And if you lose that case, it may mean the end of U.N. authority on Mars."

"Then there's just one thing to do," Johnny Coombs said. "We've got to find Roger Hunter's bonanza."

It was almost midnight when they left the major's office, a gloomy trio, walking silently up the ramp to the main concourse, heading toward the living quarters.

They had been talking with the major for hours, going

over every facet of the story, wracking their brains for the answer—but the answer had not come.

Roger Hunter had found something and hidden it so well that three groups of searchers had failed to uncover it. After seeing the gun, the major was convinced that there had indeed been a discovery made. But whatever that discovery had been, it was gone as if it had never existed, as if by some sort of magic it had been turned invisible, or conjured away to another part of the solar system.

Finally, they gave up, at least for the moment. "It has to be there," the major said wearily. "It hasn't vanished, or miraculously ceased to exist. We know he was working on one claim, one asteroid. There were no other asteroids in the region, and even the ones within a wide radius have been searched."

"It's there, all right," Tom said. "And somewhere there must be a clue."

"But what? Asteroids have stable orbits. Nobody can just make one disappear."

They called it a night, finally; the major had to complete a report for the forthcoming hearing, and the others were too weary to think any more. They felt talked out, physically and mentally drained.

On the main concourse they found a commissary store still open, and stopped for surro-steaks and coffee-mix. It was a gloomy meal. They hurried through it and rode a late jitney back to the Hunter apartment.

Once home they found more bad news waiting. There were two messages on the recordomat. The first was an official summons to appear before the United Nations Board of Investigations at nine the following morning to answer "certain charges placed against the above named persons by the

Governing Board of Jupiter Equilateral Mining Industries, and by one Merrill Tawney, plaintiff, representing said Governing Board." They listened to the plastic record twice. Then Greg tossed it down the waste chute.

The other message was addressed to Greg, from the Commanding Officer of Project Star-Jump. The message was very polite and regretful; it was also very firm. The pressure of the work there, in his absence, made it necessary for the project to suspend Greg on an indefinite leave of absence. Application for reinstatement could be made at a later date, but acceptance could not be guaranteed.

"Well, I might have expected it," Greg said, "after what the major told us. The money for Star-Jump must have been coming from somewhere, and now we know where. The company probably figures to lay claim on any star drive that's ever developed." He dropped the notice down the chute, and laughed. "I guess I really asked for it."

"You mean I pushed you into it," Tom said bitterly. "If I'd kept my big mouth shut at the very start of this thing, you'd have gone back to the project and that would have been the end of it."

Greg looked at him. "You big bum, do you think I really care?" He grinned. "Don't feel too guilty, Twin. We've been back to back on this one."

He pulled off his shirt and walked into the shower room. Johnny Coombs was already stretched out on the sofa, snoring softly. Tom sprawled in the big chair. He was tired; every muscle seemed to ache, but he was not sleepy. After a bit the shower went off and Greg stuck his head in the door. "You coming to bed?"

"Right away," Tom said, but he didn't move. The room light was dim, and his mind was back in the major's office, thinking about the strange gun, the questions without any answers, and the unpleasant prospects of the day ahead.

A hearing, maybe the first of many. Charges and counter-charges. Three men, two of them the sons of a miner who had been killed in a mining accident, all three possessed by the insane idea that an organization with the spotless reputation of Jupiter Equilateral Mining Industries, Inc., had caused that miner's death. Three men determined to revenge that death. A foolish decision, of course, but not unbelievable. Grief-stricken men had done things far more foolish in the past.

And the story the three men had to tell? A fantastic tale of a bonanza that disappeared, of a man who was murdered for something—nobody knew what, that he was supposed to have discovered—nobody knew where, and then concealed so well that nobody could find it again, not even his own sons and heirs.

Sitting there, Tom realized how perfectly incredible the story sounded. Unsubstantiated ideas, claims with no evidence to back them up—it would be bad. And with the power and funds that the company had to press the thing through—

It could be *very* bad.

But there must be an answer, if they could only see it.

Suddenly the room seemed hot and stuffy, oppressive. He couldn't think straight. Perhaps there had been too much thinking, too much speculation. Tom stood up and slipped on his jacket. He had to walk, to move about, to try to think clearly. He slipped open the door, and started for the ramp leading to the main concourse.

There had to be an answer, somewhere.

It was almost two o'clock, and the dim night lights had gone on in the concourse, replacing the bright daytime lights.

He met occasional groups of miners heading home after a late night; otherwise the concourse was deserted.

He took the up ramp, emerged at ground level, and walked along the streets under the plastic bubble. These were the oldest streets in Sun Lake City. Some of the original buildings were still here. In the dark sky he could see a vast powdering of stars, far more than anyone could ever see on Earth. He paused to watch the two brighter dots of light, Mars' tiny moons, making their way across the sky.

He went on along the steel walkways, trying to clear his mind of the doubts and questions that were plaguing him. At first he just wandered, but presently he realized that he had a destination in mind.

He went up a ramp and across the lobby of the United Nations Administration Building. He took a spur off the main corridor and came to a doorway with a small circular staircase beyond it. At the bottom of the stairs he opened a steel door and stepped into the map room.

It was a small darkened amphitheater, with a curving row of seats along one wall. On either side were film viewers and micro-readers. Curving around on the far wall, like a huge parabolic mirror, was the map.

Tom had been here many times before, and always he gasped in wonder when he saw the awesome beauty of the thing. Stepping into the map room was like stepping into the center of a huge cathedral. Here was the glowing, moving panorama of the solar system spread out before him in a breathtaking three-dimensional image. Standing here before the map it seemed as if he had suddenly become enormous and omnipotent, hanging suspended in the blackness of space and staring down at the solar system from a vantage point a million miles away.

Once, Dad had told him, there had been a great statue in the harbor of Old New York which had been a symbol of freedom for strangers coming to that city from across the sea, and a welcome for countrymen returning home. And someday, he knew, this view of the solar system would be waiting to greet Earthmen making their way home from distant stars. The map was only an image, a gift from the United Nations to the colonists on Mars, but it reproduced the solar system in the minutest detail that astronomers could make possible.

In the center, glowing like a thing alive, was the sun, the hub of the magnificent wheel. Around it, moving constantly in their orbits, were the planets, bright points of light on the velvet blackness of the screen. Each orbit was computed and held on the screen by the great computer in the vault below.

But there was more on the map than the sun and the planets, with their satellites. Tiny green lights marked the Earth-Mars and the Earth-Venus orbit ships, moving slowly across the screen. Beyond Mars, a myriad of tiny lights projected on the screen the asteroids. Without the magnifier Tom could identify the larger ones: Ceres, on the opposite side of the sun from Mars now as it moved in its orbit; smaller Juno; and Pallas; and Vesta.

For each asteroid which had been identified, and its orbit plotted, there was a pinpoint of light on the screen. For all its beauty, the map had a very useful purpose—the registry and identification of asteroid claims among the miners of Mars. Each asteroid registered as a claim showed up as a red pinpoint; unclaimed asteroids were white. But even with the advances of modern astronomy only a small percentage of the existing asteroids were on the map, for the vast majority had never been plotted.

Tom sank down in a seat and watched the map, just as he had when he was a little boy, spending hours gazing at the panorama. He knew now why he had come. To him the map had always seemed a place of refuge; he was alone here, his mind worked clearly. He could put aside unimportant things and probe to the depths of any problem. He remembered how he had loved to sit and watch, to use the magnifier to pick out obscure asteroids, to peer at Earth's moon in its endless revolutions, to imagine that he was riding the orbit ships back to Earth, or out to the moons of Jupiter.

Now he moved up to the map and activated the magnifier. Carefully he focused down on the section of the Asteroid Belt they had visited so recently. Dozens of pinpoints sprang to view, both red and white, and beneath each red light the claim number neatly registered. Tom peered at the section, searching until he found the number of Roger Hunter's last claim.

It was by itself, not a part of an asteroid cluster. He stepped up the magnification, peered at it closely. There were a dozen other pinpoints, all unclaimed, within a ten-thousand-mile radius.

But near it, nothing.

No hiding place.

And then, suddenly, he knew the answer. He stared at the map, his heart pounding in his throat. He cut the magnification, scanning a wide area. Then he widened the lens still further, and checked the co-ordinates at the bottom of the viewer.

He knew that he was right. He *had* to be right. But this was no wild dream, this was something that could be proved beyond any question of error.

Across the room he picked up the phone to Map Control. It buzzed interminably; then a sleepy voice answered.

"The map," Tom managed to say. "It's recorded on time-lapse film, isn't it?"

"'Course it is," the sleepy voice said. "Observatory has to have the record. One frame every hour."

"I've got to see some of the old film," Tom said.

"*Now*? It's three in the morning."

"I don't need the film itself, just project it for me. There's a reader here."

He gave the man the dates he wanted, Mars time. The man broke the contact, grumbling, but moments later one of the film viewers sprang to life. The map co-ordinates showed at the bottom of the screen.

Tom stared at the filmed image, the image of a segment of the Asteroid Belt the day before Roger Hunter died.

It was there. When he had looked at the map, he had seen a single red pinpoint of light, Roger Hunter's asteroid, with nothing in the heavens anywhere near it.

But on the film image taken weeks before there were two points of light. One was red, with Roger Hunter's claim number beneath it. The other was white, so close to the first that even at full magnification it was barely distinguishable.

*But it was there.*

Tom's hands were trembling with excitement; he nearly dropped the phone receiver as he punched the buttons to ring the apartment. Greg's face appeared on the screen, puffy with sleep. "What's up? Thought you were in bed."

"You've got to get down here," Tom said.

Greg blinked, wide-awake now. "What's the matter? Where are you?"

"In the map room. Wake Johnny up too and get down here. And try to get hold of the major."

"You've found something?" Greg said, excited now.

"I've found something," Tom told him. "I've found where Dad hid his strike, and I know how we can find it!"

## Chapter Fourteen

---

## THE MISSING ASTEROID

FAR out in the blackness a point of light glowed, first faintly, then brighter as the ship approached.

At that distance it could easily have been mistaken for a star, except that the ship's contact mechanism was alert for that particular point of light. The view screen caught it, flickered past it, and then returned to center in. The computer began buzzing, comparing the co-ordinates of the point of light with the co-ordinates previously computed; automatically, new fixes were taken on the sun's orange disc and on the dwindling red spot that was Mars.

When the co-ordinates matched there was a signal on the control panel. A man in United Nations patrol uniform stuck his head into the after cabin and said, "I think we've made our contact, Major."

It was an asteroid. It was not large, as asteroids go, just less than a mile in diameter, a ragged mass of stone and metal, some three billion tons of it, moving swiftly in its orbit in exactly the same way it had done for uncounted centuries.

But it was a remarkable asteroid. It even had a name. Hundreds of years before it had been spotted for the first time by Earth's astronomers; years later, when observatories on the Moon had been built, it had been observed very closely indeed, and its orbit had been carefully tracked for many decades.

And now Major Briarton and the Hunter twins crowded to the view screen, staring at the image of the tiny rock, as if they hoped, even at this distance, to fathom the secret they prayed it held.

"So this is the one," the major said finally. "How soon will we contact, Lieutenant?"

"Twenty-three minutes," the patrolman said. "Barring any trouble."

"Take your time. We want a perfect contact."

It was undoubtedly an asteroid. It grew swiftly larger in the screen, and soon Tom could make out details on the rocky surface. But this asteroid was not in the Asteroid Belt. Many hours before they had left Sun Lake City behind them, moving away from Mars in toward the orbit of Earth, to intercept a lone asteroid moving in an orbit far from its brothers.

"Hermes," the major said softly as he watched it approaching. "An eccentric. Years ago these rocks were called 'male' asteroids, all because the early astronomers were such romantic gentlemen. When the belt was first discovered, they started naming each new rock they spotted, giving them female names. The habit stuck, too, but then they discovered these few asteroids with wildly eccentric orbits, and gave them male names to keep them separate."

"But I thought it had a stable orbit," Tom said.

"It does, up to a point. It travels in an ellipse, like any planetary body, and it travels around the sun. Of course, it wobbles a bit, going in closer to the sun sometimes, and out farther sometimes, in a predictable cycle. But one thing is sure—Hermes doesn't run with the pack."

The lieutenant came back, and a signal buzzer sounded. "Better strap down now, Major. We'll have to maneuver a little."

"Any trouble?"

"Not a bit. But I take it you want to come close enough for a landing."

"That's what we want," the major said with an edge of excitement in his voice. "We want to make a landing very much."

Quickly, then, they strapped down.

It had been a wild twelve hours since Tom's call to his brother from the map room in Sun Lake City. The major had arrived first, still buttoning his shirt and wiping sleep from his eyes. Johnny and Greg came in on his heels. They found Tom waiting for them, so excited he could hardly keep his words straight.

He told them what he found, and they wondered why they had not thought of it from the first moment. "We knew there had to be an answer," Tom said. "Some place Dad could have used for a hiding place, some place nobody would even think to look. Dad must have realized that he didn't have much time. When he saw his chance, he took it."

And it was pure, lucky chance. Tom showed them the section of the map he had examined, with the pinpoint of light representing Roger Hunter's asteroid claim. Then the map control officer—much more alert when he saw Major Briarton —brought an armload of films up and loaded them into the projector. They stared at the screen, and saw the two pin-points of light where one was now.

"What was the date of this?" the major asked sharply.

"Two days before Dad died," Tom said. "There's quite a distance between them there, but watch. One frame for every hour. Watch what happens."

He began running the film, the record taken from the map itself, accurate as clockwork. The white dot was moving in toward the red dot, at a forty degree angle. For an instant it looked as though the two were colliding, and then the distance between them began to widen again. Slowly, hour by hour, the white dot was moving away, off the screen altogether.

The major looked up at Tom and slammed his fist on the chair arm. "By the ten moons of Saturn," he exploded, and then he was on his feet, shouting at the startled map control officer. "Get me Martinson down here, and fast. Call the port on a scrambled line and tell them to stand by with a ship on emergency call, with a crack interceptor pilot ready to go. Then get me the plotted orbits of every eccentric asteroid that's crossed Mars' orbit in the last two months. And double-A security on everything. We don't want to let Tawney get wind of this."

Later, while they waited, they went over it to make sure that nothing was missing. "No wonder we couldn't spot it," the major said. "We were looking for an asteroid in a standard orbit in the belt."

"But there wasn't any," Tom said. "Dad's rock was isolated, nowhere near any others. And we were so busy thinking of the thousands of rocks in normal orbits between Mars and Jupiter that we forgot that there are a few that just don't travel that way."

"Like this one." The major stared at the screen. "A long, intersecting orbit. It must swing out almost to Jupiter's orbit at one end, and come clear in to intersect Earth's orbit at the other end."

"Which means that it cuts right through the Asteroid Belt and on out again." Tom grinned. "Dad must have seen it coming, must have thought it was on collision course for a while. But he also must have realized that if he could hide something on its surface as it came near, it would be carried clear out of the belt altogether in a few days' time."

"And if we can follow it up and intercept it—" The major was on his feet, talking rapidly into the telephone. Sleep was forgotten now, nothing mattered but pinpointing a tiny bit of rock speeding through space. Within an hour the asteroid had been identified, its eccentric orbit plotted. The coordinates were taped into the computers of the waiting patrol ship, as the preparations for launching were made.

It could not be coincidence. Somewhere on the surface of that tiny planetoid racing in toward the sun they knew they would find Roger Hunter's secret.

Below them, as they watched, the jagged surface of the asteroid drew closer.

It was not round—it was far too tiny a bit of cosmic debris to have sufficient gravity to crush down rocks and round off ragged corners. It was roughly oblong in shape, and one side was sheer smooth rock surface. The other side was rough, bristling with jutting rock. More than anything else it looked like a ragged mountain top, broken off at the peak and hurled into space by an all-powerful hand.

Slowly the scout ship moved closer, braking with its forward jets. The pilot was expert. Carefully and surely he aligned the ship with the rock in speed and direction. In the acceleration cot Tom could feel only an occasional gentle tug as the power cut on and off.

Then the lieutenant said, "I think we can make a landing now, Major."

"Fine. Take a scooter down first, and carry a guy line."

They unstrapped, and changed into pressure suits. In the airlock they waited until the lieutenant touched the scooter down. Then Major Briarton nodded and they clamped their belts to the guy line.

One by one they leaped down toward the rock.

From a few miles out in space, the job of searching the surface had not appeared difficult. From the rock itself, things looked very different. There was no way, from the surface, to scan large areas, and the surface was so rough that they had to take constant care not to damage their boots or rip holes in their suits. There were hundreds of crevices and caves, half concealed by the loose rock that crumbled under their feet as they moved.

They spread out from the scooter for an hour of fruitless searching. Tom spent most of the time pulling his boots free of surface cracks and picking his way over heaps of jagged rock. None of them got farther than a hundred yards from the starting place. None of them found anything remarkable.

"We could spend weeks covering it this way," Greg said when they met at the scooter again. "Why don't I take the scooter and criss-cross the whole surface at about fifty feet? If I spot anything, I'll yell."

It seemed like a good idea. Greg strapped himself into the scooter's saddle, straddling the fuel tanks, using the hand jet to guide himself as he lifted lightly off the surface. He disappeared over the horizon of rock, then reappeared as he moved over the surface and back.

Tom and Johnny waited with the major. Twenty minutes later Greg brought the tiny craft back again. "It's no good," he said. "I've scanned the whole bright side, came as close as I dared."

"No sign of anything?" Johnny said.

"Not a thing. The dark side looks like a sheer slab, from what my lights show. If we only had some idea what we were looking for."

"Maybe you weren't close enough," Tom said. "Why not drop each of us off to take a quarter of the bright side and work our way in?"

The others agreed. Tom waited until the major and Johnny had been posted; then he hopped on the scooter behind Greg and dropped off almost at the line of darkness, where the sheer slab began. All of them had hoped that there might be a sign, something that Roger Hunter might have left to mark his cache, but if there was one, none of them spotted it. Tom checked with the others by the radio in his helmet, and started moving back toward the center of the bright side.

An hour later he was only halfway to the center, and he was nearly exhausted. At a dozen different spots he thought he had found a promising cleft in the rock, a place where something might have been concealed, but exploration of the clefts proved fruitless.

And now his confidence began to fail. Supposing he had been wrong? They knew the rock had passed very close to Roger Hunter's asteroid, the astronomical records proved that. But suppose Dad had not used it as his hiding place at all? He pulled himself around another jagged rock shelf, staring down at the rough asteroid surface beyond.

At the base of the rock shelf, something glinted in the sunlight. He leaped down, and thrust his hand into a small crevice in the rock. His hand closed on a small metal object.

It was a gun. It felt well-balanced, familiar in his hand— the revolver Dad had always carried in his gun case.

He had to let them know. He was just snapping the speaker switch when he heard a growl of static in his earphones, and then Greg's voice, high-pitched and excited:

"Over here! I think I've found something!"

It took ten minutes of scrambling over the treacherous surface to reach Greg. Tom saw his brother tugging at a huge chunk of granite that was wedged into a crevice in the rock. Tom got there just as the major and Johnny topped a rise on the other side and hurried down to them.

The rock gave way, rolling aside, and Greg reached down into the crevice. Tom leaned over to help him. Between them they lifted out the thing that had been wedged down beneath the boulder.

It was a metal cylinder, four feet long, two feet wide, and bluntly tapered at either end. In the sunlight it gleamed like polished silver, but they could see a hairline break in the metal encircling the center portion.

They had found Roger Hunter's bonanza.


In the cabin of the scout ship they broke the cylinder open into two perfect halves. It came apart easily, a shell of paper-thin but remarkably strong metal, protecting the tightly packed contents.

There was no question what the cylinder was, even though there was nothing inside that looked even slightly familiar at first examination. There were several hundred very tiny thin discs of metal that fit on the spindle of a small instrument

that was packed with them. There were spools of film, thin
as tissue but amazingly strong. Examined against the light
in the cabin, the film seemed to carry no image at all. But
there was another small machine that accepted the loose end
of the film, and a series of lenses that glowed brightly with
no apparent source of power. There was a thick block of shiny
metal covered on one side with almost invisible scratches.

A time capsule, beyond doubt. A confusing treasure, at
first glance, but the idea was perfectly clear. A hard shell
of metal protecting the records collected inside.

*Protecting against what? A planetary explosion? Some sort
of cosmic disaster that had blown a planet and its people
into the fragments that now filled the Asteroid Belt?*

At the bottom of the cylinder was a small tube of metal.
They examined it carefully, trying to guess what it was supposed to be. At the bottom was a tiny stud. When they
pressed it, the cylinder began to expand and unfold, layer
upon layer of thin glistening metallic material that spread
out into a sheet that stretched halfway across the cabin.

They stared down at it. The metal seemed to have a life
of its own, glowing and glinting, focusing light into pinpoints
on its surface.

It was a map.

At one side, a glowing ball with a fiery corona, an unmistakable symbol that any intelligent creature in the universe
that was able to perceive it at all would recognize as a star.
Around it, in clearly marked orbits, ten planets. The third
planet had a single satellite, the fourth two tiny ones, the
sixth eleven. The seventh planet had ten, and was encircled
by glowing rings.

The fifth planet was broken into four parts.

Beyond the tenth planet there was nothing across a vast

expanse of the map, but at the far side was another star symbol, this one a double star with four planetary bodies.

They stared at the glowing map, speechless. There could be no mistaking the meaning of the thing that lay before them, marked in symbols that could mean only one thing to any intelligence that could recognize stars and planets.

In the center of the sheet was another symbol. It lay half-way between the two solar systems, in the depths of inter-stellar space. It was a tiny picture, a silvery sliver of light, but it too was unmistakable.

It could be nothing else but a star ship.

Later, as they talked, they saw that the map had told each of them, individually, the same thing. "They had a star-drive," Tom said. "Whatever kind of creatures they were, and what-ever the disaster that threatened their planet, they had a star-drive to take them out of the solar system to another star."

"But why leave a record?" Greg wanted to know. "If no-body was here to use it."

"Maybe for the same reason that Earthmen bury time cap-sules with records of their civilization," Major Briarton said. "I'd guess that the records here will tell, when they have been studied and deciphered. Perhaps there was already some sign of intelligent life developing elsewhere in the solar sys-tem. Perhaps they hoped that some of their own people would survive. But they had a star-drive, so some of them must have escaped. And with the record here—"

"We may be able to follow them," Greg said.

"If we can decipher the record," Johnny Coombs said. "But we don't have any clue to their language."

"Did you have any trouble understanding what the map had to say?" the major said quietly.

"No."

"I don't think the rest will be much more difficult. They were intelligent creatures. The record will be understandable, all right." He started to fold the map back into a tube again. "Maybe Roger Hunter tried to use the film projector. We'll never know. But he must have realized that he had discovered the secret of a star-drive. He realized that the United Nations should be the ones to explore and use it, and he gave his life to keep it out of the hands of Tawney and his men."

"A pity," a cold voice said close behind them, "that he didn't succeed, after all."

They whirled. In the hatchway to the after cabin Merrill Tawney was standing, with a smile on his lips and a Markheim stunner trained directly on Major Briarton's chest.

## Chapter Fifteen

### THE FINAL MOVE

FOR a moment they could only stare at Tawney's smiling face. Then the lieutenant made a swift move. *"Don't try it,"* Tawney snapped, tightening his finger on the trigger. "I'm an excellent shot. One more move from any of you, and the major will learn what stun-shock feels like."

Swiftly the little company man crossed the cabin, motioning them together against the wall with his stunner. He reached out to the radio panel, flipped it open, and expertly ripped out a handful of wiring. Then he leaned back against the control board, smiling again. "I realize I'm much earlier than you expected, Major. You did a very neat job of camouflaging your takeoff. We were almost fooled, and no doubt the dummy ship you sent off later got full fanfare. I suppose there will be a dozen patrol ships converging on this spot in a few hours, expecting to surprise a Jupiter Equilateral ship making a desperate attempt to hijack your little treasure here."

The fat man laughed cheerfully. "Unfortunately for you,"

he went on, "we have many friends on Mars, including a man in the map room. I'm afraid your little trap isn't going to work after all."

The major's face was gray. "How did you get here?"

"By hitch-hiking. How else? Most uncomfortable, back there, even with a pile of pressure suits for padding, but your pilot was really very skillful."

Johnny Coombs turned on the major. "What does he mean, a trap? I don't get this."

The major sighed wearily. "I had to try to force his hand. Even if we found what we were looking for, we had no case that could stand up against them. We needed *proof,* and I thought that with this as bait we could trap them. He's right about the patrol ships, but they won't be near for hours."

"And that will be a little late to help," Tawney said pleasantly.

The major glared at him. "Maybe so, but you've gone too far this time. This is an official U.N. ship. You'll never be able to go back to Mars."

"Really?" the fat man said. "And why not? Officially I'm on Mars right now, with plenty of people to swear to the fact." He chuckled. "You seem to forget that little matter of proof, Major. When your patrol ships find a gutted ship and five corpses, they may suspect that something more than an accident was involved, but what can they prove? Nothing more than they could prove in the case of Roger Hunter's accident. Scout ships have been known to explode before."

He ran his hand over the metal cylinder. "And as for this, it's really a surprise. Of course when we failed to find any evidence of mining activity, we were certain that Roger Hunter's bonanza was something more than a vein of ore, but *this!*" He looked at their long faces. "Don't worry, it will all be over quickly. My ship will be here in minutes now, and as soon as we have transferred your little treasure, we won't make you suffer any longer. And you can be certain that we will exploit the secret of a star-drive to the very fullest."

"How do you think you can get away with it?" the major said. "Turning up with something like that right after a whole series of suspicious accidents in space?"

"Oh, we aren't as impatient as some people. We wouldn't be so foolish as to break the news now. Five years from now, maybe ten years, one of our orbit ships will happen upon a silvery capsule on one of our asteroid claims, that's all. I wouldn't be surprised if a non-company observer might be on board at the time, maybe even a visiting senator from Earth. For something this big, we can afford to be patient."

There was silence in the little scout ship cabin. They knew that Tawney meant everything he said. For all his smiling conversation, he was alert, and the weapon in his hand did not waver. A single false move would just bring the inevitable that much sooner.

And the end seemed inevitable. This was a desperate move on Tawney's part. He was gambling everything on it; he would not take the chance of letting any of them return to Mars or anywhere else to testify.

As soon as Tawney's ship arrived, it would all be over.

Greg caught Tom's eye, saw the hopelessness on his brother's face. He clenched his fists angrily. If it were not for Tom, Dad's bonanza might have gone on circling the sun for centuries, maybe forever, wedged in its hiding place on the rocky surface of the eccentric asteroid.

But it had been found. Earth needed a star-drive badly; a few more years, and the need would be desperate. And if a group of power-hungry men could control a star-drive and hold it for profit, they could blackmail an entire planet for centuries, and build an empire in space that could never be broken.

He knew that it must not happen that way. Dad had died to prevent it. Now it was up to them.

Greg glanced quickly around the cabin, searching for some way out, something that might give them a chance. His eyes stopped on the control panel, and he sucked in his breath, his heart pounding. A possibility.

It would require a swift, sure move, and someone to help, someone with fast reflexes. It was dangerous; they might all be killed. But if his training at Star-Jump was good for anything, it might work.

He caught Johnny Coombs' eye, winked cautiously. A frown creased Johnny's forehead. He shot a quick look at Tawney, then lowered his eyelid a fraction of an inch. Greg could see the muscles of his shoulders tightening.

Greg took quick stock of the cabin again. Then he took a deep breath and bellowed, "Johnny! *Duck!*"

Almost by reflex, Johnny Coombs hurled himself to the floor. Tawney swung the gun around. There was an ugly ripping sound as the stunner fired, but Greg was moving by then. In two bounds he was at the control panel. He hooked an arm around a shock bar, and slammed the drive switch on full.

There was a roar from below as the engines fired. Greg felt a jolt of pain as the acceleration jerked at his arm. Tom and the major were slammed back against a bulkhead, then fell in a heap on top of Johnny and the lieutenant as the awful force of acceleration dragged them back. Across the cabin Tawney sprawled on the floor. The stunner flew from his hand and crashed against the rear bulkhead.

On the panel Greg could see the acceleration gauge climbing swiftly—past four g's, up to five, to six. The ship was moving wildly; there was no pilot, no course.

With all the strength he could muster Greg tightened his arm on the shock bar, lifting his other arm slowly toward the cut-off switch. He had spent many hours in the acceleration centrifuge at Star-Jump, learning to withstand and handle enormous forces of acceleration for brief periods, but the needle was still climbing and he knew he could not hold on long. His fingers touched the control panel. He strained, inching them up toward the switch.

His fingers closed on the stud, and he pulled. The engine roar ceased. On the floor behind him Tawney moved sluggishly, trying to sit up. Blood was dripping from his nose. He was still too stunned to know what had happened.

Greg leaped across the room, caught up the stunner, and then sank to the floor panting. "All right," he said as his breath came back, "that's all. Your ship may have trouble finding us now, but I bet our pilot can get us back to Mars."

When they left the Sun Lake City infirmary it was almost noon, and the red sun was gleaming down from overhead. Walking slowly, the Hunter twins moved along the surface street toward the U.N. building.

"He'll recover without any trouble," the doctor assured them. "He caught the stunner beam in the shoulder, and it will be a while before he can use it, but Johnny Coombs will be hard to keep down."

They had promised Johnny to return later. They had had check-ups themselves. Tom's eyes were surrounded by purple splotches, and his broken left arm was in a sling. Greg's arms and legs were so stiff he could hardly move them. The major and the lieutenant were sore but uninjured.

Now the boys walked without talking. Already a U.N. linguist was at work on the record tapes from the metal cylinder, and a mathematician was doing a preliminary survey on the math symbols on the metal block.

"I hope there's no trouble reading them," Greg said.

"There won't be. It'll take time, but the records are decipherable. And Dr. Raymond was certain that the engineering can be figured out. Earth is going to get her star-drive, all right."

"Well, one thing's sure—there'll be some changes made, with the U.N. moving out into the belt," Greg said. "And we've got work to do."

"You mean the trial?" Tom said. "I guess. The major says that Jupiter Equilateral is trying to pin the whole thing on Tawney now. But they won't get away with it, if we can stand together on our story of what happened."

Greg looked at his brother and grinned. "You know something, Twin?" he said. "I don't think we're going to have much trouble standing together from now on about anything."

Somewhere in the distance the twins heard the rumble of engines. They stopped and watched as a great silvery cargo ship rose from the space port and headed up into the dark blue sky. They watched it until it disappeared from sight.

They were both thinking the same thing.

An Earth-bound ship, powerful and beautiful, limited now to the sun and nine planets, unable to reach farther out.

But some day soon a different kind of ship would rise.